Dedicated to all those who served in war and peace and their family who waited for them.

CAMP HELL

CHAPTER 1

A Four man Navy Seal team was slowly making their way through a battlefield; they are making their way toward the Prime Minister's house. There were two drug cartels fighting to take over the country of Enceladus and they would kill anyone standing in their way, they needed to control the city in order to set up base camp and run drugs into the United State and other countries.

The team had been ordered to get the Prime Minister and his family and take them to the airport, out of the country and to safety. The American Ambassador and his stuff were going to meet them at the airport, if they could get there. One of the two drug cartels that were fighting here for control of drug trade here was run by a guy named Chavez, and he wanted them all of dead. Chavez was a real nut a little loco, if you did not share in his beliefs you were dead or just simply disappeared. Once they got to the Prime Minister's house they saw at least four soldiers already deceased and you could tell that they had put up one heck of a fight. One man was in a business suit and died in the doorway with gun in hand and after closer inspection they realized that it was the Prime Minister. They radioed in that the Prime Minister was gone and that four men were down at the scene, they quickly paid their respects even thought the same thought crossed all of their minds, you never leave a soldier behind, however getting them out was going to have to wait. Suddenly they heard crying softly inside of the building the Navy Seal's carefully entered and in the hallway close to the door they found a badly wounded female with a pistol drawn. She slowly lowered her gun as soon as she knew that they were Navy Seal's. Sitting next to her was a young girl about fifteen years old who was trying to stop the bleeding; the cloth she was using was soaked up in blood.

The woman reached up with her bloody hand and grabbed Master Chief John O'Donnell shirt, "Please get my daughter Rose to America, where she will be safe."

John looked at the young girl and then back at the woman and saw that she was too now was deceased and even though she would not hear him he answered aloud as not alarm the girl any further, "I give you my word that she will be safe." He reached out and closed her eyes and then spoke to the girl, "We are leaving NOW, and grab whatever you can carry!"

Chief Paul Blue put his hand to his earpiece, "Their plane can't land to retrieve them, there is just too much heavy fighting at the airport sir, and they can't wait for use so they are stealing an airplane!"

John looked at his men, "Looks like we need to go to plan B."

Chief Jimmy Johnson looked at John and he rolled his eyes, "I was afraid you were going to say that."

John gave them a little laugh, "Sam, you take the lead, then Jimmy me and then Rose, Paul you take up the rear. It's important that I get back home, my girlfriend told me in her last letter that she had a big surprise waiting for me when I get back."

Jimmy gave John a large smile, "That redhead you met six months ago is going to be the death of you yet." Then he slapped John on the back and laughed at him as he headed out.

Rose gave her mother a kiss on the forehead and then followed Sam out of the building, she stopped briefly at her lifeless father's side closed her eyes and said a quick prayer for him, but not before John stopped and put a stick of Juicy Fruit gum on the door and a note that said, "Juicy Fruit was here."

She then followed Sam until they came to the edge of town and then headed into the woods. The rest of the team followed closely behind with their weapons ready.

Sam pulled out a machete and starting hacking his way though the thick brush of the forest. When they heard a low flying airplane they looked up and saw a plane was on fire and going down.

Rose watched the plane until it was out of sight; everyone hoped that no one on the ground would be hurt when it crashed since that was inevitable. Rose fought back some more tears; she was very scared and unsure what was going to happen to her once she left this place, she had heard Chavez shouting that he was coming back and when he did he would kill her. She watched as all of the Navy Seals now using their machetes so they could move faster, then they reached a narrow path. They fallowed the path for a while until they heard some loud voices arguing up ahead and the smell of burning fuel.

John had the group just crouch down in the brush as he and Sam slowly moved forward looked through the trees and saw the crashed airplane. There was a small group of men who were arguing very loudly and one man was lying on the ground with an injured leg. Sam started to move forward but John put his arm on his shoulder and shook his head no, with a wide smile on his face. Sam just shook his head and headed back to the group. He knew that John had one of his crazy ideas again and that could only mean one thing trouble, if it goes bad.

Once back with the group, John got down on one knee and gave everyone a large smile, "It looks like the airplane that we saw going down a little bit ago is up head and it had on board it the Ambassador, his staff and a few others. I want to teach them a little lesson for making so much noise in a war zone." Everyone in his group just rolled their eyes, but Rose looked very confused, she did not understand what was going on.

John looked at Rose, "Put on your best dress." He then pulled out a hand grenade, took the top off and poured the gun power out and then put the top back on. Rose pulled a very fancy dress over her head adorned with a scarf and a bonnet; he could tell she was not happy to be doing this.

Rose walked up to the Navy Seals and knelt down next to John, "I had planned on wearing this when I got to America."

John smiled at her, "Don't you worry about that, and I will buy you some nice clothes to wear when we get you there alone with a big fancy dress." He looked at the rest of his team and then back at Rose, he handed the grenade to her, "Give us a few minutes to work our way around them and then throw the hand grenade as close as you can to them. If any one goes near it, you step out and ask them to please return your favorite hand grenade or should the Navy Seals behind you shoot?"

Rose just looked at the hand grenade in her hand and then nodded her head as she watched them move into the forest beyond view and then turned and looked at the men who seemed to taunting each other to fight.

Lt. Commander Ben Mahoney and Major Mike Rohrer were facing each other with their fists raised as if they are ready to duke it out over whose idea was best.

They both looked down at the injured man as the doctor tried to stop the bleeding, Rohrer then took one step closer to Mahoney, "I say we take him back to the city and get him some help."

Mahoney just shook his head no as he got into Rohrer's face, "That is a bad idea Major, they tried to kill us the last time we were in the city, or have you forgotten that?"

Abruptly they heard Lance Corporal Robert Bowden shouted, "HAND GRANADE!"

Rohrer jumped toward the downed plane as Mahoney just froze; he then looked down at his feet and saw the hand grenade. Of course he spotted that the pin was still in it, so he bent over and picked it up to throw it back at whoever made that mistake, but before he could pull the pin he saw a young girl who looked like she was on her way to some fancy tea party and she has her hand out toward him.

Rose felt a little silly and scared as she saw the man looking at her bewildered, and she saw some other men in the doorway to the plane, stunned. "Could I please have my favorite hand grenade back, or do I have the Navy Seals shoot you?"

Everyone heard Bowden shout, "Do as she says there are four of them behind us!"

Mahoney slowly looked over his shoulder and then very gently flipped the hand grenade back to Rose and then raised his hands over his head.

Rohrer seeing who they were came stormy out of the airplane shouting as he made his way up to the Navy Seals, "WHAT THE HELL DO YOU THING YOUR ARE DOING?"

John just walked by ignoring him, then he approached Bowden and Sam (a/k/a Runner), "Runner, see what you can do for him?"

Sam just nodded his head, he knew that John want them to use code names for safety reasons, he opened his first aid kit and got down next to Bowden to attend to his wounds, he then heard a man near him, "Give me that, I'm a doctor." None of John's men had names on their uniforms so if anything went bad, no one could trace them back to the United States.

Doctor Dale Thompson grabbed the knife out of Sam's hand and started to pull things out of the kit as fast as he could, Rose knelt down beside him, "Can I help too?"

John just gave Rohrer a smirk; "We are the guys that are going to get your sorry Asses out of here, if you keep your voices down. Now everyone exit the plane so we know how many of you there are?"

Rohrer angrily moved right up into John's face, "I want your names and ranks, I'm going to file a report on all of you about what you did here today, it was recluse, dangerous and just plan uncalled for!" Not seeing any names on their uniform or any kind of rank.

John grinned then just ignored Rohrer as he watched three other men come out of the plane, they all looked okay but one, he look hurt and was being helped by the other two. Then John looked back at Rohrer, "Uncalled for, is that your professional report sir? Be careful General, you are really beginning to annoy me and that makes me angry, and you wouldn't like me when I'm angry."

Rohrer started seeing red and grabbed the front of John's shirt, "It's Major Mike Rohrer, I'm not a General yet!" Rohrer was so mad at John he was shaking; he never saw this fist that hit him.

John just turned and looked at one of the men standing near the down airplane, "Major, you help the Admiral here carry the General we have to leave here, now!" John then looked at Mahoney who was just staring down at Rohrer who was out cold and winked.

Major Sam Cook slowly walked toward Rohrer and he kept one eye on him, he was thinking that this guy was unpredictable, or just plain crazy.

John turned and motioned toward Paul Blue, "Check the plane and see if there is anything in it we can use to carry this guy with as he pointed toward Bowden."

Paul moved into the airplane and looked inside he saw lots of bundles all over the plane and he had a bad feeling about this plane. Not making any assumptions he addressed one of the men near the plane, "What is in those bundles?"

One of the men leaned against one of the other men, "Heroin."

John pointed at Jimmy, "Firecracker, set up some of your explosive devises and set the timers to go off about a half hour after we leave here."

Jimmy took some explosive devises out of his pack and got to work on it. The whole team hated drug dealers and anyone who helped them. It took him only about five minutes to set them up, no one who entered the plane after they left would see them under some of the bundles. Stepping out of the plane he saw that Rose was wrapping her scarf around Bowden's leg and trying to help him.

John looked back the way they had come in and took a mental note about the rest of their surroundings he didn't want to wait much longer, who knows how many saw the plane go down and how far away they were. He also knew the drugs were someone's and that they would be looking to retrieve them. He saw Jimmy exit the plane and he too was looking around a bit concerned. John then gave the word, "All right, let get moving, I do not want to be trapped here, Fire cracker take point."

Half hour later they entered a big clearing, just as they heard a very loud explosion coming from where the plane was, and it was followed by some gunfire. John motioned for everyone to get down, and then called for the radio, "Juicy fruit calling Mickey Mouse."

After a little static and a couple more call outs they all heard the static break with a voice, "Juicy Fruit this is Mickey Mouse responding, what can we do for you?"

John just smiled, as he looked at everyone else who seemed a bit puzzled, "I need an immediate EVAC of my team and others and we are being pursued by enemies who are heavily armed."

Some chuckles came from the radio, "When is there not something or someone chasing after you Juicy fruit? What do you need us to do this time?"

John tried not to laugh, "I need one of your special whirly birds and anything else you may have around to pick us up, some are in need of some medical attention ASAP."

Ten minutes later two black hawk helicopters and one Marine Osprey helicopter appeared over the tree line, one of the black hawks landed, and so did the Marine Osprey. The other black hawk just hovered near the tree line behind them, John pointed at the Marine Osprey helicopter, "That your ride gentlemen." John then waved his men and Rose toward the other black hawk, "Let's go men, I have a hot date waiting for me."

Just as the helicopter were about to take off the other black hawk that was keeping watch opened fire upon someone or something in the forest until both helicopters were in the air and moving away from the area.

Four hours later Rohrer and Mahoney were standing in front of a two-star General, who was reading their reports and Rohrer was still rubbing his jaw. General Owen set the reports down and then looked up at them. General Owen then took a deep breath, "If I were you Rohrer I would just forget it, if you were to have him arrested, he could come up with at least ten men who would swear he was with them playing cards at the time. As for getting his real name and rank the same goes for any of his men, you do not have the security clearance high enough yet to get that information at this time."

Rohrer leaned forward putting his hands on the deck, "I do not care anything about clearance, and I want him arrested right now for hitting me."

Owen pointed toward his stars on his shoulder, "Even I do not have the clearance to get his name or rank. I have been told by my superiors that it would be best for your career that you just leave it lie, unless you do not care about your career, he saved all of your lives, just remember that." Then he pointed at the door, "Dismissed." He then put the report into a shredder next to his deck as he watched them leave his office.

Two days later John was exiting an airplane in Washington DC with his men when he spotted a very pregnant redheaded Navy officer, the guys started to tease him, "I told you she would be trouble, John, yea she had a surprise waiting for you alright."

John dropped his head and just slowly walked toward her remembering what his mother had said many years ago about getting a gal pregnant without marrying her first; those words were starting to haunt him as he approached her and why didn't kids listen to what they were told when they were younger?

Margie Bender just walked right up to John and gave him big hug and then pointed at her rather large stomach, "Wow, so this was your surprise, I didn't think I was gong that long," she gave him a crooked look, "Twins, I have a hotel room waiting for us, let's go I missed you a lot."

John just stared at Margie for a moment and couldn't take his eyes off of her stomach, "Okay but no more sex until after we are married."

All of John's men could not believe what they heard next and from a female Navy officer, I think they actually started to blush, as they turned they saw John just standing there with his hands on his hips and a large grin on his face, I mean let face it, it was a little late for the no sex part.

John just stood there and listened to her for a good two minutes before she stopped to catch her breath and then he grabbed her and embraced her in a deep long kiss, "Let's find a minister and get married as fast as we can, I want to be with you."

Margie just grabbed a hold of John's arm and all but dragged him toward a waiting car as his men just shook their heads, they knew he was about to get married whether wanting to really or not and he now was definitely off the market.

CHAPTER 2

Eighteen years have passed and Sergeant John "O'Donnell slowly shook his head a few times trying to clear it as he tried to get up again for the third time, but as before when he got half way up he was hit again on the back of his head. This time he raised his head enough to get a glance at whom was hitting him over and over again, this was not his idea of fun filled afternoon. Through his bloody right eye he saw a man in a fancy business suit standing over him, he had a menacing grin on his face and a large club in his hand, then he saw his face, he was President Chavez and off to his side was Marines, Lieutenant Jim Brown and Lieutenant Jack Brown, both were taking delight in his pain. The last time he had seen them they were collecting a lot of money divided into two brief cases from two Enceladus officers. From the look of it he didn't make it back to the ship to report what he had seen to his own Marine and Naval officers on the U.S.S. Bataan. He knew that his reflexes were not as good as they were when he was young and that is why he left the Seals and joins the Marines.

President Chavez brushed some of the dirt off of his shirt and pants as he took a step closer to John and looked down at him sneering, "So you think I'm nuts or crazy for my beliefs and for the about people and for the way I run my country, right Sergeant?"

John just turned his head and looked down and before anyone realized he lurched forward at both of the Brown's, he was beyond caring at this point in his life. Before he could get within a foot of them, he was hit in the back of his head by something again he dropped to the ground again but not out.

Chavez walked over to John and with the tip of his shoe rolled him over, "For your crimes, you will spend the rest of your life in this prison camp and if you think these officers will become sympathetic and will help you, you are sadly mistaken they are my amigos and let's just say help me in my business." Turning to his left he pointed at another man in rags who was on his knees, this man was terrified, he knew what was going to happen to him, "This man tried to escape and there is a penalty for that, I will draw ten names out of a barrel to be executed by the guards here any way they choose!" He waved his hand at some guards who were pulling a barrel toward him. He chuckled under his breath. The barrel had a lot of pieces of paper in it, and John knew each one represented a life. Chavez slowly walked up to it and then motioned to another guard who had a computer tablet in his hand, the guard started typing and it was then that John saw a large number of people many dressed in rags being pushed out of a building that looked worn and ready to fall down, some were just kids, some looked sick, and many also knew what was going to happen here.

The ground in front of the man who was on his knees, slowly started to open and flames shot up out of the ground. Chavez walked over behind the man, draw out his pistol and shot the man in the back of his head; the man's lifeless body fell into the fire pit. He then walked over to the barrel and opened a small panel, he reached in and started to pull out pieces of paper, and then read off the names one by one. The guards upon hearing the names walked over to each prisoner and pushed them toward the fire pit, one guard grabbed a baby out of a mother's arms, carried it over to the fire pit and threw it in alive, a great cackle came from his lips as the woman screamed in horror the others tried to comfort her. The prisoners whose names were called were forced onto their knees, in front of the pit, and then shot in back of their head one by one their lifeless bodies fell into the pit. Once they have all been killed, the pit, started to closes, but the woman who had the baby taken from her ran up to the fire pit and jumped into it screaming her child's name, then all was silent.

John was about to jump up and attack Chavez when he saw a pistol in front of his face and Lieutenant Jim Brown laughed at him in a nauseating way, "You can't out run a bullet Sergeant, do you want to die here? By the way, this camp is surround by a very large mine field, and there is only one way in or out."

Chavez slowly walked back toward John as he put his pistol away and stopped short, "I understand you were a Navy Seal for quite a few years. Maybe you can help me find a Navy Seal who went by the code name Juicy fruit. I want to know his real name and where I can find him. He took something of mine and I want it back! You give me his real name, and after he arrives you will be free to leave, and go home to your lovely family."

John tried not to laugh but he was laughing on the inside, he knew that it was not what he took, but whom he helped to escape from this country over 18 years ago. He spit out a tooth and then looked up at Chavez with a toothless smile, "I have never heard of him, even if I did I would never betray a fellow Navy Seal!"

Chavez put his hands on his hips and started to turn away but not before he kicked John hard in the head knocking him out cold and knocking out another tooth.

A short time later John woke up inside of a building, it was in pretty bad shape and looked like it was ready to fall down at any moment. He slowly got up onto his knees and looked around. There were a lot of people there, everyone who was sitting near him was in bad shape and some were just kids. It was then that he saw that many of the kids here had birth defects of one kind or another. They were all dirty with unkempt hair you could see that they had been there a while; they were all just wearing rages. One of the prisoners was an older women; she looked at him with a frown. He rubbed his head a bit because he now felt a headache coming on, he spoke to the older women, "Who is in charge here?" He decided to get a bit more comfortable and sat down on his ass. Looking around the room he saw no furniture or walls separating areas of any kind, just a dirt floor. There was a foul smell coming form somewhere.

Raeanne Romani just shock her head and put her head in her hands she was desperate as she watched her young daughter Mary Romani slowly walking toward them, "There is no one person who is in charge here, every time someone does try to lead us, the guards beat them severely or just kill them, they don't want us gathering or planning. So everyone here has given up trying to be in charge of us here at camp HELL that is what this place is called."

John just looked around the room again and then stood up and waved his arms for everyone to come closer to him. He felt his blood start to get hot, his face turning red and an unmistakable anger starting to build up inside of him, but he fought it down, he needed to know more about this place first. Once everyone had moved close to him calmly put his hands on his hips in a non-threatening manner, "Starting to day, I'm taking charge of things here, and I know that it's a risk, but I am willing to take that risk. My first order of business is to tell you that no one tries to escape unless we all escape!" Seeing a lot of puzzled faces, he then said the same thing in Spanish, it was a little rusty but he saw some smiles this time. "I also want someone to fill me in on what is going on here so I can help if I can." He saw that the building was in need of repairs terribly and the roof had a hole in it and if not fixed soon it probably would get bigger, if the building didn't fall down first. Then he spotted an older man slowly heading toward him he looked like he had on an old uniform, it definitely looked like it had seen better days.

The man stuck out his right hand, "My name is Pablo Robertson and I was a general in the Enceladus army that was, until I tried to over throw Chavez two years ago. If you want, I will fill you in about this place and what we do here?" Both of them then sat down on the dirt floor as Pablo began to fill him in on everything on the inner workings of the camp.

For the next two hours Pablo told him about the camp and John just got more angrier by the minute he could not believe what was happening, camp hell indeed. He was told that the guards would rape and torture and humiliate prisoners and make everyone watch, Chavez even had videotaped the goings on for leverage that was he could blackmail anyone who got out of line. During the day they worked in poppy fields, drugs were the business of choice for the cartel, and some days they worked in caves at an archaeology site a mile away from the camp, those days were a welcome distraction. But it was the drug business that Chavez and his two Lieutenants were into the most and made the most money at. Pablo waved his head toward a man looking out of the windows and told John that his name was Mahari Guerra and he once was a doctor until he could not save Chavez's wife when she had fallen ill and had a heart attack Chavez had his hand smashed and off to camp hell he went. They also have a priest they called father Campbell who said the wrong thing in his church one-day, Chavez had the church burned to the ground and he was sent here too, it was a crime to speck out about Chavez or any of the cartels under his command.

John just shook his head in disbelief as he continued to listen to one story after another and all had similar fates. All Chavez cared about was the drug money. Looking at Pablo, "One of the first things I want to do here is keep the walls from collapsing, how can we going about this?"

Pablo just gave him a little laugh, "You can ask the guards but they will just laugh at you, they do not like to spend money on us, just look at we have to wear. When our clothes wear we are naked, they don't care just as long as we keep working! The only bathroom we have is a pit outside with a plank across it, and the guards have to stand watch, it is so uncomfortable especially for the ladies. At night we just use the far corner if we have to go, so that we are protected, we can't trust the guards at night. Once a month we clean it out that is why it smells in here.

John looked down at his hands, then back up and around at everyone, "Then we will just have to use what is in here, I do know a little bit about building and fixing things, my wife does a lot of building in the Navy as she is a Navy Seabee."

Pablo look at John with a little smile, "I'm glad that if you are taking charge here, they will not listen to me because they do not trust me, of course

I cannot blame them I did work for Chavez for a while. I'm only here because I tried to stop him and his men from killing the doctor after his wife died, I mean he worked so hard to try and save her life. That is when I tried to over throw him or so he has told everyone here."

John looked over at the doctor and then back at Pablo and laughed, "I knew he was a nut case, I just didn't know how bad."

John stood up and waved everyone to come closer to him and looked down at Pablo, "Could you help me? My Spanish is not that good, only if you think they will trust you to speak for me?"

Pablo stood up next to John and told everyone that John wished for him to translate for him, and once they understood that John started to tell them a few things.

The next morning John led the prisoners out of the building and had them line up the way he had told them the night before, the older people in front and the youngest in the back with some of the older ones on each side too, he wanted to protect the younger ones by placing them in the middle. He watched as the guards slowly started to count them, he was trying to figure out who was in charge and just how many there were. He also took a good look around at all of the buildings and the guard towers that surrounded the camp and paid attention to which ones were manned and unmanned. He counted six guard towers and each one has one man on watch and he counted fifteen guards on the ground. One of the guards walked to the front of the prisoners with a clipboard in his hand and a club in the other with a broad smile.

Hallmar stopped in front of John; "I can see who is in charge of my prisoners now, so I'm going to tell you what is going to happen today. First they are going to be lead out to our fields to work on the seeding and tilling, second they will then pick the flowers that are ready to be picked and finally if they pick enough to our satisfaction, they will be fed when they get done later today."

John tried to stand up straight, "They would work better and longer if they were fed first."

Hallmar just looked over his shoulder at some of the other guards who were laughing and then turned back toward John and without warning swung his club and struck John on top of his right shoulder, whish knocked him down to his knees. Then he looked down at John on the ground. John slowly got back up rubbing his shoulder, "They eat when we say they can eat and not before Sergeant, do you hear me!" Without warning Hallmar swung he club again and hit John on top of his right shoulder again knocking him back to the ground. Then he turned toward his soldiers and laughed loudly as John slowly got back up onto his feet not saying a word.

John got up and rubbed his shoulder more, he thought long and hard about hitting Hallmar back, and boy he wanted to so badly he could taste it, but he did not want to see any of the other prisoners get hurt today on his account. He looked over his left shoulder, "Have it your way, then."

Hallmar then turned and waved at the guards who were at the main gate and they slowly pulled it open then he turned back to John and said with a grin, "Lets get to work today it going to be a hot day."

Ten hours later John slowly led the prisoners back into the camp and most of them were barely moving, they were exhausted from picking, working in the hot sun all day without any breaks. John had a large knot on the side of his head, from earlier when he asked for some gloves to wear while working in the poppy field.

He spotted a large black kettle on the back of a truck bed and his stomach felt empty, it had been a long time since he had eaten, the last time was on the ship.

Pablo moved up next to him and whispered, *"Be careful there is never enough for everyone to eat and sometime the food is bad too."*

John turned and looked over his shoulder at everyone who was behind him, most didn't look good and they knew some would not get fed today. He gave the guards a look of disdain and then looked back at the ones behind him. "Pablo, have the kids line up first, I want the youngest to eat first and then the older ones, I will eat last.

So that is the way it went for the next two months and it was hard work, but finally after a while he found a way for everyone to get something to eat on the days they were fed. The one thing he hated the most was the food was the same thing everyday, cold bean tacos and sometimes there were bugs in it, but who was going to complain when you're starving.

CHAPTER 3

Meanwhile on the U.S.S. Bataan Lieutenant Jack Brown was standing in front of the Captain Paul Bearden with a picture in his hand of a crocodile with a Marine boot in its jaws, on the picture was a lot of blood and bone. "They say he fell off of a cliff and fell into the river below and this was all they found when they went down to find his body, Sir."

Captain Paul Bearden looked at the picture, he became pale, but knew he had to hold it together so he took a deep breath, "Then that's it, he's dead and we can leave here and head home."

Lieutenant Brown stood up at attention, "Sir, if you want I will notify his wife and kids?"

Captain Bearden just shook his head, "No, I will forward this to the Pentagon and they will notify them properly."

The next day little John Jr. and his twin sister Sandy O'Donnell were coming home from collage and saw two Navy officers and another gentleman leaving their home. Little John and his sister looked at each other bolted into their house and saw their mother sitting on the sofa crying holding a picture and some papers.

Margie O'Donnell looked up at her children as she wiped some tears off from her face and held out the picture, "They said your father is dead, but if you look closely at the picture, you will see that it is not his boot! But they will not believe me, this boot looks about a size 9 or so but your father wore a size 12 boot. I should know since most of the time I bought your fathers gear for him, the difference is huge."

Little John just grab the picture out of his mother's hand and looked at it and then showed it to his sister, "Anyone can see that this boot is way too small to be dad's boot, they should examine it closer!"

Margie slowly stood up and finished wiping the tears from her face, "That is what I tried to tell them, but they said they had a witness that said your dad fell off of the cliff and into the jaws of this crocodiles that were at the base of the cliff." She held up the piece of paper that was given to her by the officers that were there, "I will not sign this sheet of paper to get his death benefits until I have seen his body, not just one of his allege boots!" She sat back down and put her head into her hands, "On top of all this I just found out earlier today that I am pregnant, and it's a girl."

Little John and Sandy beamed with excitement, "Dad will be so happy and excited, and everything will be fine." Then Sandy sat down next to her mother and put her arm around her mother, "What do you want us to do to help you?"

Margie just looked up the of both of them, she was so proud of the both of them, "Just want what your dad wanted, you two to go to collage and make something out of your lives. So you have something you can do besides serving in the Military. Your father has spilled enough blood for this country. But if that is the path you choose your father and I will support anything you decide to do. As for me, I'm going to retire from the Navy and take over my dad's constriction company, God knows he has been asking me to do for the last three years."

Little John looked down at his mother, "If you want, I will put off collage for a few years to help you out?"

Margie stood up fast and without thinking blurted out, "NO, you will keep going to collage that was your father's dream and mine too, so do not argue with me over this!" She then turned and looking at Sandy who had also stood up, "You know it was our dream as well as yours that you to become a Pediatric doctor that is your passion."

Sandy looked at her brother and then her mother, "Can we talk about this for a bit?"

Margie's eyes got wide, "NO, so it will not do any good to argue with me." Not waiting for them to keep arguing with her she turned and walked out of the room.

Little John just looked at his sister; "You think we should tell her we are joining the ROTC, at the collages we are going to?"

Sandy slowly shock her head no, "She would not be happy about that right now, this is not the time, but she will understand that it is in our blood to serve this country, just like mom and dad and our grandparents did and those who have come before them too."

He gave his sister a little smile, "I have decided that I am going to join the Marine, I will find dad and find out why they want us to believe he is dead."

Sandy gave her twin bother a little smile, "You have always been extremely ambitious like dad, dad always told me there were not enough Pediatric doctors in the Navy, so that is what I'm going to do."

Little John tried not to laugh, "We can't tell mom our plans for at least a year, she has enough to worry about especially if she is taking over grandpa's business and has a new baby on the way."

CHAPTER 4

Three months later Sergeant John O'Donnell and the rest of the prisoners have just returned from the poppy fields they were so tired their bones ached and the guard have just refused to feed them today relaying that they did not work hard enough. John sat down near the barrack entrance and looked down at these hands, all he saw were blisters on top of blisters. He was still having a hard time getting used to being a leader to all of the prisoners but for some reason they trusted him to look after them and to help them when he could. He had started having them do some light stretching when they got up in the morning; it was a necessary evil to keep them from getting to stiff. One thing he is kind of happy about is that he had managed to get one of the guard's to give them a soccer ball on days they do not have to work in the poppy fields.

John looked up saw Raeanne and her daughter Mary walking toward him, Mary was looking toward the front gate as a car slowly approached it and Raeanne almost looked sick and very pale. Raeanne sat down next to John as Mary kept an eye on the car as it entered the camp then she took one step inside of the barrack. Raeanne put her hand on John's shoulder, "It's those Lieutenants that were here three months ago, this time they have returned and I have a feeling they are after Mary. Last time they were here they ran out of time, that was the day they brought you here and they said they would be back but they had to get to he ship and collect their drug money. They come here about every two to three months on their way to get it."

John just looked up a bit and watched as the car come to a stop just inside of the gate and those two bastards got out and started to head his way. For the first time he saw that they were warning General uniforms with five stars on the collar. He just slowly shook his head and felt his argue slowly start to get the better of him; it rose all the way up from his toes. He thought he heard the old soldiers sprits and ancestors who had gone before him encourage him to do nothing at this time. He hated it when they told him to do something that he did not want to do. They had gotten him into more situations then he care to remember when he was younger and all they would say was that it was a prelude for things to come later in his life. When the two were about ten feet from them he slowly started to get up and tried to block them from seeing Mary who had moved into the back of the barracks. Again he heard those voices inside telling him to not do anything crazy, *"John you don't need to die today."* Of course at this point in his life John was beyond caring it seemed that this was more important then being rational at this time.

Lieutenant Jim Brown looked at his brother as they approached John with smiles on their faces; John took a few steps closer to them. Lieutenant Jack Brown walked over to one of the guards and whispered something to him that guard raised his weapon and held it on John.

John had a bad feeling about this and he watched the Lieutenants movements out of the corner of his eye. He saw that many of the guards were walking toward them, some carrying clubs and laughing. Up in one of the windows of the guard towers he saw a man with a video camera and then made him more livid.

Jim looked at Raeanne, who was trying to hide behind John, "Raeanne, your older daughter

Angella is string up more trouble for President Chavez again in the United Stated." Jim stared at John, "We do not believe that you do not know who Juicy Fruit is. You were a Navy Seal for a very long time, and now you are here, tell me who he is." John kept silent "MARY, come out here we have something special planned for you today."

Mary very slowly came out of the barrack's, she knew what was going to happen was not going to be good, she had long ago given up trying to fight the men here. She was not willing to look at her mother or John, she crept closer to them and kelp her hands hidden behind her back because she didn't want the guards to see that she had one long and sharp fingernail on each hand. Her sister Angella had always told her to keep one that way just in case someone ever tried to get at her, she needed to find a way to scar them for life. She knew that whoever she marked would probably kill her though, so as she approached them the only thing going through her mind was, was she ready to die today. Or would she rather be raped in front of everyone. She just hoped it would be over fast.

Jack moved over next to his brother and put his hand on his brother's shoulder as he looked at Mary and licked his lips, then he looked at John. "We have something special planned for you today, Sergeant. You get to be the one who is going to have Mary today!"

Jim gave Mary an evil smile, "Get yourself prepared little lady?

John slowly got to his feet and tried not to look at Mary and just fixated his stare on the guards, Mary was looking at John with sad eyes, knowing that he was a good man. John stood up straight and just stared at both of the brothers, as he shook his head no, "NEVER, I do not rape anyone, I'm a Marine!"

Jack walked up to John and reached out take John's arm, but John just broke free and stood even taller and stared straight ahead. He then heard those voices in his head telling him today was not a good day to die.

Raeanne lovingly looked up at John, in the short time she had known him she knew he would give his life to all of the prisoners here, and she also knew that once he made up his mind, there was no changing it.   She slowly stood up herself went up to John and put her hand gently on his elbow, "Please, they will kill you if you do not do as they tell you, just make it quick, and I know you will be gentile, they would not."

John did not move but clenched his fist and still stared straight ahead, as if he had not heard her and then he shook his head no again.

Jack looked at his brother, this was going to take a little more enticing then he thought, and without warning drove his right fist into John's stomach as hard as he could as he stepped back John doubled over but did not fall down. John took a breath clenched his teeth and stood back up straight again and looked straight ahead.

Jack monition for two of the guards to come over and they both grabbed John's arms and all but dragged John toward Mary, now Mary had a look of shock on her face, she could not believe what was happing, she thought no one that was exhausted and starving would have the strength to fight for her. This was the last thing she had expected to happen to her today.

One of the guards swung his club at John, hitting him on the shoulder knocking him down onto the ground and one kicked him in the side with his boot. John shook his head a few times, he was a bit dazed and when he looked up he thought he saw two of his old Soldier spirits and some ghostly figures of old Marine Sergeant's telling him to get back up. One of the ghosts he swore was an old Navy Seal instructor of his holding a bell and a box of donuts, now he was thinking this must be a nightmare, but he was still awake. So doing as instructed he stood back up and just stared straight ahead, he spit out another tooth, but he spit it toward Jack, hitting him on the nose, he would have laughed if he didn't hurt so bad at the time.

Jack looked down at the tooth that had fallen to the ground wiped off his nose and suddenly swung his fist at John again, and broking his nose, it knocked him back a bit but not down. Jack was now livid he grabbed the front of John's shirt with a crazed look on his face, "I was not going tell you this but since you are so set on dying today, I will. Your wife and kids were killed in a car accident after a night of drinking, they ran head on into the front of a big truck doing a hundred mile an hour!"

Hearing this news John just smiled at him, his wife did not drink and would never speed, in fact he teased his wife about being so careful about the speed limit it had become an inside endearing joke, but even though he did not believe this, he lost it anyway, he was just plain madder then hell at this point and fed up, he headed straight toward Jack, all he saw was red, he was beyond caring at this point, "Kill me, just kill me and get it over with." Before he could even get close enough to inflict harm on Jack he was hit again by two of the guards with clubs one hit him on the top of his shoulder and the other across his back, knocking him down again. Jack and Jim both joined the guards with their clubs and continued kicking and punching.

Mary could not believe her eyes as she watched John take a beating over and over and every time it stopped he stood up again. Mary was thinking why doesn't he just stay down? But it just continued and he wasn't even fighting back any more as if he wanted to die today, it was honor. Mary looked around all of the other prisoners they had gathered around by now and she saw shock and pride on all of their faces. They needed John; he had made their lives bearable. Mary decided that he was too important and her mind was made up, she knew what she had to do, she would not let him die today, they need him alive.

Mary got up and knelt down beside him and took his hands, "Please."

Jim looked at Mary as he delivered one more kick to John, "Look Sergeant, she wants you, why fight it you might even enjoy it."

John shook his head no a few times and got back up and tried to stand at attention, again he heard in his mind the sprites yelling at him to stand be a man.

Mary looked at the other prisoner's and their eyes were pleading with her to do something, if he were to die today, who would stand up for them and teach then how to survive here, she remembered what it was like before he was there. Watching John again knocked to the ground she looked over at her mother, her mother gave her a nod and then she called out the names of five male prisoners' took a step toward John and motions to them.

The five men moved toward John just as he is about to get up again and they grabbed him and pushed him back down toward the ground. "Please do not fight any more we do not want you to die, you are the most honorable man I have ever met!"

Though his blooding eyes, John still stared at the guards and tried to get back up but had no strength left they carried him over to Mary and out of respect all of the prisoner's turned their backs to them.

Three hours later John was sitting inside of the barracks' in a back corner, with his head in his hands as he cried softly and Mary was trying to talk to him, "I'm sorry but I could not let them kill you, as we need you alive."

Waving her away he buried his head deeper into his hands, "Leave me alone for a while, I don't want to talk to anyone right now."

Mary sat down next to him she also shed tears, "Listen I'm scared too, and I could get pregnant, I mean there is not birth control here, but I would rather have you be it father then one of those guards. The last time the Lieutenant got someone pregnant they killed them both as soon as they found out about it."

Pablo moved over and sat down on the other side of John and put his arm around his shoulder, "Listen Sergeant, you do not know how much we have come to counting on you these last few months to keep us alive."

John just waved them away he still did not want to talk to anyone today he was having a hard time dealing with had just transpired, especially being filmed and the guilt he felt was weighing heavily on his heart.

CHAPTER 5

Nine months later John lift up a baby girl to the night sky with tears in his eyes, "Soldiers and ancestors who have gone before, this is my daughter and her name is Janet lightfoot O'Donnell. I do not know what your plans are for her, but please keep her safe." He lowered his baby girl and bent over handing the baby back to Mary

Mary took the baby girl to her breasts and with tearful twinkle in her eyes, "Thank you for naming her."

John then took off his rag that used to be a shirt, "Use this as a diaper for as long as you can, I will try to find other resources." He then moved to a space in the barracks under part of the open roof and sat down. He wanted to look up at the stars and he wanted to let the tears fall but he knew that he could not show that side of him to the others, he needed privacy and some time to think and talk to the spirits. "What do you want from me? What you want me to do now, give me a sign?" He waited, but nothing happened, they would only appear to him when they were damn good and ready so he retuned back to his sleeping spot and sat down deep in thought.

Robertson sat down next to John and he too looked up at the stars, "You have to be strong now Sergeant, both of them need you more then ever now."

John just nodding his head a few times and then looked at Robertson, "But there is only so much that I can take!"

Putting his arm around John, "The lord will not give you more then you can handle, my son."

John gave Robertson a broad smile, "It's the sprits of the ones who have gone before me that I see, and I worry about them the most, sometimes they want me to do crazy things with no warning,

and I sometimes question if I should follow."
Robertson listened as John explained further and
tried to comfort him, "It is like believing in God,
sometimes he too asks things of us that we
question."

The next morning they were told that they were
not working; half of the guards were absent doing
something for President Chavez.

Later that day while most of the kids were
playing soccer in the yard, a truck came down the
winding road leading to the front gate. All of the
kids stopped playing and headed back into the
barracks as the truck pulled to the stop. The back
of the truck was facing the barracks and two guards
jumped out of the truck and ran to the back and
dropped the tail gate, then two more guards
jumped down out of the back with guns drawn.

John has a bad feeling about this, and all he
could do was watch as all of the occupants of the
truck were thrown out onto the ground, a young
female about nineteen or twenty, followed by three
teenager boys and then another female who looked
a little older, both women looked like hell, their
clothes were in tatters. Next to come out of the back
of the truck were five men, and they looked to be
sailors but from where John was not sure. The
older female slowly got up off of the ground and
looked around she was definitely scared then
spotted John and the rest of the prisoners. The
younger one got up much faster she looked as

though she wanted to fight, but hesitated for a moment and just looked at her surroundings she then got behind the men trying to hide herself, she seemed a little self-conscious as she picked at her clothes trying to straighten then out.

Hallmar walked up to the new prisoners and then turned and looked at John, "Sergeant, I will let you to tell these new prisoners what the rules are here." Then he walked away. He motioned for the truck to move away and back toward the gate.

John saw the young girl start to move toward Hallmar, so he moved in-between her and Hallmar who was just standing there smiling at her. "Everyone come with me and no one will get hurt today!" John rounded up the new prisoners toward the back corner of the barracks, but glanced over his shoulder at Hallmar who just stared at John. He winked at John, which just pissed him off.

Once he had gotten them all together in the barracks he whistled to get their attention. They were all scared and nervous and listened intently. John put his hands on his hips and slowly looked them over. "First of all I am going to tell you that I'm in charge of all of the prisoners here and second of all do not get the guards mad at you no matter what. Just go along with things the best you can, if you need to speak to someone speak to me, third of all the guards love to hurt people rape and video tape things, I will do the best I can to keep you safe, but remember I too am a prisoner here. My name is Sergeant John O'Donnell and I'm a US Marine. If you are thinking about escaping forget about it, I will not allow it unless we all escape at once. If you think anyone is going to come to your rescue forget about it, no one knows that you are here, as far as anyone knows you are all dead! If you listen to me I will do my best to keep you alive while you are here." He knew that what he had just told them, hadn't sunk in completely, they were too frightened so there would be many questions later, but he was prepared to answer.

They then looked around at the other prisoners and got a feel for their new surroundings. All hope for rescue was gone you could see in their mannerisms that they had given into the life they were about to live, the other prisoners slowly moved closer to them to greet them and introduce themselves.

Diane Mahoney slowly moved up to the new prisoners, "My dad is an Admiral in the U.S. Navy and he will come looking for me!"

John took a step closer to Diane with his arms crossed in front of him, "First tell me your dad's name, I might know him, then tell me what happened, how you came to be here?"

Diane looked over her shoulder at the sailors, "His name is Admiral Ben Mahoney! We were on a ship doing some research for the United Nations on the water near here, when all at once a patrol boat came alone side of us and boarded us, we had no reason to turn them away because we thought they were friendly. They then killed our Captain and second officer when they tried to take over the ship. They force us onto their boat and sank ours, next thing we knew they brought us here after they stopped and pick up these others." She pointed toward the teenager.

John was upset at the story she had just told, and shook his head, "So your dad finally made Admiral, but not even an Admiral can save you if no one knows where you are." He then addressed the teenagers, "What's your story?"

Marie Otto slowly moved in front of the other teenagers, "My name is Marie and we are going to college until President Chavez closed it, we decided to go and talk to him about reopening it again. But all he did was turn us over to those men two other girls were killed when they resisted, then they brought us here with the others after they burned the school down."

John again shook his head, "You now know what kind of people we are dealing with and you know what they are capable of doing." He looked at Diane and then the rest of the new prisoners, "Tell me a little bit about yourselves?"

Diane first looked at the others and then took a step forward, "I was a teacher for five years until I got burned out, and so then joined the United Nation working on water issues around the world until they captured us." The rest were scientists and Marie and her fellow students were studying agriculture.

John slowly looked them over sadly, "Diane you and the other from the collage will be teachers here at night if that is okay with you and the others. The more we educate ourselves the more we can work on preparations for things to come. I need help keeping everyone's minds sharp and off of the hell going on here and more on what we can do to survive, we have a lot of young ones here and they need something to occupy their time."

Diane took one step closer to John with a puzzled look on her face, "Did you not hear me, and I got burned out teaching? What are we supposed to teach them and what with?"

John walked up to Diane, raised his hand and pointed other forehead, "This is all you need to teach these kids and some of the adults too, and if you have not noticed this is not a classroom."

Diane reached up and swatted his hand away from her forehead and started to say something but was stopped when she heard Mary, "If you want to stay alive, you will listen to him and do what he says."

Diane looked over at Mary, who was standing near the doorway to the barrack holding Janet close to her chest her eyes were hollow and sad. "Who are you to tell us what we can and cannot do?"

Mary looked at her baby and then back at the rest of the new prisoners, "I have been here a very long time and I have seen it all. I know what the guards and the others who come here will do to you if you do not listen to Sergeant. He is the father of my daughter, and not by choice, that alone should give you just cause to listen."

Diane took a few steps closer to Mary, "You mean his is your husband?"

Mary looked at John and then at Diane tears started to well up in her eyes, "NO, I had to force myself upon him to keep him alive or they would have killed him!"

CHAPTER 6

Five years later Little Bear and his cousin's Nighthawk and Sleeping Dog had just finished Seal camp, they were waiting for their first assignment while visiting their Indian Reservation in Arizona. Sleeping Bear saw a ten-year-old boy running up to them almost out of breathe, "Your father just came out of the sweat lodge after forty-five minutes, he even needed the help of your stepmother Barbara the Wild she wolf! He told me to get something out of his house for him." Without another word he was off and running again without looking back at them.

Little Bear looked at his cousin with a worried look on his face and then they bolted off toward sweet lodge. When they arrived, they saw his dad Big Bear on the ground in his stepmother's arms.

Barbara looked very concerned and she was she was cradle Big Bear in her arms. She was holding a bottle of water up to his mouth trying to get him to drink.

Little Bear dropped down onto his knees right in front of his dad and grabbed his arm, "Dad are you alright?" He looked up at Barbara, "What was he doing in the sweet lodge for that long?"

Without taking her eyes off of her husband, "I just found out he was in it for that long so do not blame me for this!"

Big Bear reached out and put his hand on his son's hand, "Do not blame her my son, it was the sprites of our ancestors and some that were unknown to me that would not let me leave until they had told me what you needed to know." Giving his wife a weak smile, he looked back at Little Bear; "You must keep your eyes open for she with one arm and the two in the box! You must save them no matter what the great white chief says and you must also take Shamus the medicine women with you when you make that night jump, my son, into a place the sprites called hell camp."

Just then the boy ran up to Little Bear caring a box that was about nine inches long and only three inches wide and handed it to him, Little Bear in return handed it to Big Bear. Big Bear reached out and grabbed the box out of Little Bears hands and opened it. Inside was an eight-inch-long knife with a buffalo's horn for a handle and it looked very sharp. Big Bear took the knife out of the case and held it up showing it to Little Bear, "This is a warrior knife, and only a warrior can handle it. That which makes this blade fell from the sky five hundred years ago in a meteorite and our ancestor found it and forged it into this knife. It had been use to defend our family, our people, and our country in battle and it has always stood true, it has been handed down from generation to generation. Today I hand it to you as the ancestor have told me during my journey in the sweet lodge. They said that I should give it to you for your upcoming battle. They have also told me that when the time comes, you need to be able to wield the knife and throw it at the enemy, they said that it will be a distance of at least fifteen paces, this will be to save your family and your other family the ones you have that are Navy Sea's!"

Little Bear reached out and took the knife from his father and held it in his hands, he could not keep from just staring at first, then he looked at his dad, "I know the story of the knife and its history, you have told it to me many time. But I do not understand what you mean by my family and the others which I call family, and does it have anything to do with John O'Donnell?"

Big Bear looked down for a moment and then back up at Little Bear, "They did not say, all they told me was to look for she with one hand and the two in the box to save your children and all of the other children." He then turned and looked at his wife, "Take me to our home for I am in the need of rest, my wife."

Barbara helped her husband rise, "I know your wisdom is beyond this world, but you most be careful."

Little Bear watched his stepmother help his dad up, and was concerned for his heath; he was not so young anymore. He used to be a great warrior, and not so long ago. She was the tribal attorney and realized she was in love with Big Bear even though he was much older then her, twenty years in fact Little Bear smiled as he watched them slowly walk toward home and away form them, then he again looked down at the knife in his hand. There were some bales of hay near the sweet lodge, so he walked to within fifteen paces and threw the knife at it, at first the knife was all over the place and nowhere near dead center, but thought a lot of practice he became very accurate.

CHAPTER 7

One year later everyone was heading back to the camp from the poppy fields, hoping that would get fed today. They were met by Jim and Jack the two guarding the camp at all times, as John had started calling them the fake generals, but not to their faces of course. They were both laughing and pushing each other around they may even been a little drunk or high, the way they were stumbling around. Lieutenant Jim Brown had a sword in his hands.

Lieutenant Jim Brown gave his brother a little playful push, and then licked his lips watching as the prisoners headed back to the camp. The same thought crossed their minds, that they had a little surprise for Mary. Jim gave his brother a toothy grin, "Remember I get her first, then you can have her."

Jack looked at his brother a sneer rose across his face, as they continued watching, "I just want to see that bastard's face when he sees what we have planned for his Mary today!"

Jim was slowly running his finger over the blade of his sword as waited for all of the prisoners to line up in front of their barracks. He saw that Mary and her little girl were standing next to that bastard Sergeant.

Hallmar Walked up to the two brothers, "Good evening my Generals, I hope you had a good safe trip?

Still looking toward the prisoner Jim then turned and gave Hallmar a broad smile, "Yes it was a good trip and once we leave here will we be picking up our money, but first we wanted to leave a present for that Sergeant if you don't mind?"

Hallmar just gave them both a loud laugh, "Why would I mind, she is still young?" He turned and looked toward the prisoners and shouted, "MARY, come over here as the generals would like to see you, NOW!"

Mary slowly moved out in front of the other prisoners she had just told her grandmother this morning that she feared that she might have cancer.

Mary had a lot of spunk and was not afraid to say what she thought, she also was not afraid to die as long as it wasn't slow and agonizing. She walked right up to Hallmar and didn't even look at the brothers, and then they went and stood where the two generals and then turning and walking over to the where the two generals were. She knew what was about to happen and even though there was fear in her voices she tried to sound as gruff as possible, "What do you want today?"

Jim pointed his sword at her face, "On your knees bitch!"

Mary kelp her eyes on the point of the sword and slowly got down onto her knees, in her mind she had already planned on what she was going to do.

Jim took a step back and dropped his pants and then walked back up to Mary an evil grin was painted on his face, "You know what I want you to do BITCH, so get at it!" He set his sword on her shoulder and moved a bit closer to her.

Mary looked up at Jim and then glanced over at her daughter and John who has put his hand on Janet's shoulder as they were all horrified, but couldn't stop watching. Then she shouted as loud as she could, "Semper Fi." Opening her mouth baring her teeth she then bit down as hard as she could.

Jim yelled out a painful scream, and took a step back, put both of his hands on the handle of the sword and raised it high over his head.

He swung his sword and took off Mary's head; Jim looked down at Mary's severed head and watches as her body fell.

John covered Janet's eyes with his hands just before it happened, he didn't want his daughter to see this, and not child should. He started to move forward but was stopped by Raeanne who whispered to him, *"Its too late to help her now! Think of your daughter."*

Jim looked up from Mary's body and looked over at John, "Sergeant you and your half-breed daughter are alone now and clean this mess up."

John slowly took a step forward took his daughter and handed her to Raeanne, "I WILL, clean that up myself!"

Jim looked at his bloody sword, and then realized he had been severely injured and needed medical attention. Jack went over and picked up the head and then looked at t John. "SERGEANT, carry this to the fire pit or I will just leave it here for a few days on a stick."

John still felt Raeanne's hand on his elbow, *"Just make it quick and do not start anything, I will explain why she did it later."*

John slowly started to pick up Mary's head he kelp his eyes on Jim who was waiting for the doctor, all he wanted to do was put his hands around his stinking neck.

Jim looked over at his brother with a wide smile and looked at John and Janet, "This is small enough for your half-breed daughter can carry this to the fire pit!"

Cursing under his breath he looked down at Janet, *"Try not to look and carry it to the pit while I carry her body."* Bending over he picked up the head and held it by the hair putting it in his daughter's hand while she looked away and then he picked up Mary's dead body and carried it toward the fire pit. John dropped Mary body into the fire pit and watched Janet drop her mother's head into the fire pit.   Not waiting for the pit to close up John reached down and took Janet by the hand and led her back to the rest of the prisoners, he spotted a video camera on the top floor of the guard's building.   Again cursing under his breath he made a promise to himself that everyone would pay for this and all of the other thinks that have happen here to the prisoners.

CHAPTER 8

Four months later Lieutenant Amy Becker was standing on the gangway to the U.S.S. Nokomis she just smiled to herself, I mean she had worked so hard to get here, and to fly a CH-53E Super Stallion off the deck of an aircraft carrier and was following her dream. Looking toward the entrance to the Nokomis when she spotted Admiral Ben Mahoney standing waiting to meet his new crewmembers. She wondered if he would recognize her or should she just keep her mouth shut about there past together, sometimes it is just better to never tell anyone about her past. She grabbed her duffle bag and headed toward the entranceway to the U.S.S. Nokomis and her life as a Super Stallion pilot. As she stepped onto the gangway she spotted over her shoulder an older Marine Sergeant and a young

Lance Corporal and right next to them was an older and younger woman. Standing in front of the older Sergeant was a young girl about six year old and she is wearing a scarf around her neck and it looked very familiar, it is then she spotted her family neck and it looked very familiar it was then that she spotted her family crest on it. Trying not to laugh she took a deep breath and then headed up the gang way stepped up to the Admiral and gave him a salute and with her Brooklyn accent, "Sir it good to see you again, Sir."

Admiral Mahoney returned her salute and with a puzzled look on his face, "Have we met somewhere before? I do not remember ever meeting you."

Amy just gave him a little smile, "Sir, if you do not remember and I was to tell you, I would have to put a bullet between your eyes and I do not think your wife Katie would like that Sir." Not waiting for him to answer she turned and walked inside.

Admiral Mahoney just watched Lieutenant. Becker walks away as he made a mental note to check her file to find out where they had met before. Then he turned back toward the gangway and smile as he watched Sergeant Major Robert Bowden and his son walking up the gangway, he knew him very well. He crossed his arms and shook his head, "Look what the cat has drug in? What is an old timer like you doing here?"

Bowden dropped his duff bag and tried his best to look angry, but failed, "Old, you say? You should talk. I can still out soldier any Marine or Navy man and twice on Sunday!" They both started to laugh. They both looked back and noticed two vans pulling up a Marine a woman who was pregnant followed by an older woman and a young girl got out of one of them. "Someone has to teach these new youngsters how us Marines do things on these Navy ships." He just nodded his head toward the young Marine, who was hugging his pregnant wife goodbye.

Admiral Mahoney walked to the edge of the gangway and smiled as he watched Margie hug her son Lieutenant John O'Donnell Jr. then John hugged his wife and his little sister goodbye. He then walked over and shook the hands of four Navy men who got out of the other Van; there was also a female Navy doctor and a young girl. Margie walked over and gave her daughter a hug as they watched the men start boarding the ship.

Admiral Mahoney turned and looked at Sergeant Robert Bowden, "That is our old friend Juicy fruit's wife and son, Lieutenant John O'Donnell Jr. I found out who Juicy fruit was three years ago and he is now missing in actions."

Robert Bowden watched as everyone was saying their goodbyes and could not believe he was finely meeting Juicy fruit's family, he gave his gratitude to Juicy Fruits wife and son and told then how heroic he was and that he saved his life all those years ago.

Margie finished giving her son a hug and then stepped back and wiped a tear off her face, "Now you be safe and listen to the other officers, you hear me son!" She then grabbed the front of his shirt and giving him another hug.

John took a step back and gave his mother and little sister Susan a big smile, "I will mom and Sister you look after mom."

Susan gave her big brother a salute being silly as always, "Yes Sir."

Just then they see a Van pulled up to the pier and three of Little John's cousin got out and give them a wave. They then also saw Little John's sister Sandy get out with another Navy Seal named Charlie Brown and a young girl named Anita who was about six years old. He gave Sandy a little kiss and then she waved at her mom, big brother and little sister.

They all watched as Little John and his cousin walk up the gangway with little John in the lead. Margie and Susan walked over to Sandy and Anita who is wiping a tear off of her face as she watched her dad walking up the gangway.

Sandy walked up to her mother and gave her a hug then turned and looked up at Charlie, "I told him I would give him my answers if I would marry him the next time I saw him."

Margie just looked up at the men as they were entering the U.S.S. Nokomis and then put her arm around his daughter, "Just remember you will have many sleepless nights, when he is gone way on missions."

Wiping another tear off her face as she looked down at Anita, "I know mom, but I had a good teacher and I do love him and his little girl with all of my heart, mom."

Margie pulled her daughter closer and she waved the little girl over to them as she watched everyone enter the U.S.S. Nokomis. The last time she had watched someone she loved enter a ship, he never came back years ago, but deep in her heart she has the feeling he will be coming back home someday. Putting her hand onto Anita's shoulder, "Your father will be ok as this is just a short cruise of just four months."

Anita turned and looked up at Margie and then at Sandy, "I pray you will say yes so I can finally started calling you my mom."

Margie gave Sandy an evil eye, "I hope you are being careful?"

Sandy tries not to laugh, "Mom, I'm a doctor and when I get married my wedding photo's will not show my stomach out to here." Holding her hands out front of her stomach.

Margie put both of her hands on her hips, "I was not out that far!"

Susan, moved up next to her big sister, 'Yes you were mom, I have seen your wedding photo's of you and dad on your wedding day."

CHAPTER 9

Angella Romani sat up fast on her cot in her jail cell in prison from of sound of machine gun fire outside of the jailhouse. It took her a moment to fully wake and then she got up and walked toward the front of her cell, wondering who was getting shot today. But instead of just the normal one or two shots the firing went on for a good minute before it stopped, then she heard two single shots. She looked around her cell and still had a hard time believing she was thought of as a threat coming back home by President Chavez.
He had baited her with the promise of talk about maybe sharing power or holding new election.

But no sooner had she stepped off the bus with her followers, they were all arrested and put in prison without a trial over four months ago.

She put both of her hands on the cell bars she called out the names of everyone in her cellblock to see if any of them were executed today? Hearing all of the people in her cellblock answer her call, she began to wonder who was shot today and why the rapid fire? Normally when someone got executed, there was no rapid fire like she heard this morning.

Everyone in the cellblock heard some angry shouting coming from the enters to the cellblock and doors being opening loudly, followed by guard named Roberto Lee who came in fumbling with his keys as he walked up to Angella's cell, he was being followed by five officers who do not look too happy.

Roberto looked over his shoulder at the officers before he opened Angella's cell door and then stepped back a few paces trying to make himself as small as he could to move out of the way.

Once Angella's cell door was open one of the officers walked up to her door and pulled out a sheet of paper, "Are you Angella Romani?"

Angella stood up, as straight as could as she could and her ears were ringing from the machine gun fire a few minutes ago, "Yes I'm Angella Romani."

The officer turned to one of the other officers with his hands outstretched and the other officer handed him a thick black book. He then turned back toward Angella and held it out toward Angella "Would you like to be sworn in as the acting President of Enceladus? Until we can hold new elections to elect a new President."

She tried not to laugh to loud and raised her right hand to her mouth, "I think that President Chavez might have something to say about that, Sir!"

All of the officers started to giggle. The officer holding the book answered her, "Did you not hear the shooting this morning? The dead cannot object to you becoming acting President."

Angella eyes get very wide, it just dawned on her that it was President Chavez who was one of those shot this morning and maybe a few of his followers. Looking at the officer who was standing in front of her holding the book she realized that it was a bible in his hand. She took a deep breath and took one step toward the officer and raised her hand right hand and placed the left on top of the bible.

Lieutenant Rafael Lang lowered the bible after Angella had took the oath of office as President, he then turned and nodded toward Roberto who moved toward some of the other jail cell and started to unlock them one by one. Then Lieutenant Lang moved closer to Angella, "I now must tell you some sad news, first your sister is dead, but your mother and your niece are still alive in camp Hell!"

Angella took a step back with a look of shock on her face, "My niece, what niece what happened?"

Lieutenant Lang glanced at the other officers for a moment then began to explain, "They are being held at prison camp the prisoners affection ally calls camp Hell, there is maybe up to 400 prisoners, a lot of them are children under the age of 10, we have video to show you of your sister, your niece and who your niece's father is.

Angella staggered back a bit, "What happened to my mother and sister, why were they sent there? What happen to my sister's husband? Last time I saw her she as to young to have a baby!"

Lieutenant Lang looked sad as he observed the other prisoners who were walking toward them, you could see that they were very happy to be out of their cells. He waved all of the prisoners to come closer to them, "You all might want to hear what I have to say before you leave here, there are a lot of lives at stake if word gets out that President Chavez is dead!"

Angella looked right at Lieutenant Rafael sternly, "I want to see those videos before we do anything!"

Rafael looked at Angella, you could see the mixed emotions on his face, and he was sad but angry "They are at the President palace, Chavez was loco, he loved to watch all of the video's the guards make at the camp."

Angella looked at her fellow prisoners, "Could you stay here until I have seen the video's. We would not want to get any of the prisoners killed, if word was to get out that Chavez is dead!" All of them understood, and agreed.

CHAPTER 10

Three hours later as Ambassador Adam Flannigan and Sergeant Joe Pederson were working on top of the American Embassy roof on the air condition unit for the forth time this year. Sergeant Pederson who was in his mid-fifty's threw down his screwdriver, "That's it, it's dead!" Ambassador Flannigan was stone face, "Maybe we should just pay President Chavez to find one of the two new units we order last year but never got here?"

Adam leaned on the dead unit and just shook his head as he took a step back and kick the dead unit a few times then he took a handkerchief out of his back pocket and wiped his forehead, "I'm past the point of caring how much he wants to find them, I'm going to find a way to pay him and to hell with Washington and their paperwork!"

Before either of them could say another word a young Marine guard about nineteen had climbed up the ladder, "Ambassador, we just got word that the President is on the way here, he will be in in five minutes or less." He saluted quickly at the Ambassador and the old Sergeant and rapidly climbed back down the ladder, he did not want to be put on KP again in this heat.

Adam and Joe headed toward the ladder together, both were not smiling at all, Adam started to go down first, "I think I can come up with at least fifty dollars, how about you and your staff?"

Joe just chuckled, "Let's ask if he will take a check, I'm sick of this hot weather, so are most of my staff who are counting down the day until they get out of this stinking hell hole! I'm still surprised he let us back into this rotten country after he kicked us out 18 years ago!" Joe followed Adam down the ladder he looked over his shoulder and saw the front gate being opened by two of the embassy guards, one was a young female guard named sergeant Samarth Black, she was on her first deployment as an embassy guard.

Once they were on the ground they both headed toward the long black car that had just entered the compound, there were armed guards on both running boards of the car. The guards did not get off their running boards until the gate was closed. No one could see in the car with the tinted windows, finally one of the guards opened the back door to the car.

The first person out of the black car was an officer, who did a quick sweep around the compound, and he was carrying a briefcase, then a woman emerged and walked right up to Ambassador Flannigan. "My name is Angella Romani, I'm the acting President of Enceladus, President Chavez is dead, he was executed early this morning, along with all of his officers and staff!" Holding up a CD box, "I have something you need to see, I need your help to save over 400 people and from what I can tell 3 are America's!" Not waiting for a response from them she walked right into the embassy followed by two officers who had came with her, you could tell they were visually upset.

Flannigan looked at Joe quite puzzled as he followed Angella into the embassy, Joe followed but had a real unsettling feeling.

Angella fought back tears as she waited for the Ambassador to come in, she looked around the embassy, for the first time wondered if this was a good idea, but she had no choice if she wanted to save all of those prisoners being held including her mother and her niece. She saw that the man walking in with the Ambassador was a Marine Sergeant and she walked right up to him "Is it true that Marines never leave a man behind?"

Joe stood up as straight as he can, "Yes, that is correct Mama."

Angella looked over at the Ambassador and then back at the Sergeant, "One of the prisoner is a Marine Sergeant and he has been held in the camp for over seven years." Holding up the DVD's again, "These are videos of this Sergeant and what they have been doing to him and a few others at the camp he is at." Looking around the room she noticed the staff were all standing waiting to see the horrors and atrocities they knew were coming. "One more thing, if the guards at the camp find out President Chavez is dead they will start killing the prisoners, before we can find a way to get them out!"

Lieutenant Lang held up his briefcase; "I have a map of the camp and some photos of some of the prisoners who are in the camp, along with pictures of the guards."

Flannigan pointed toward his office, "I have a DVD player in here and a direct line to Washington D.C. if we need to call someone, if what you are saying is true, we will have to inform them."

Once in the room Lang opened his briefcase and started to set out pictures and a large map of the camp. Joe looked down at the pictures and his eyes got wide with recognition, he then reached down and picked up one of the photos. Even with long hair and an unkempt beard he recognized the man in the picture he was startled for a moment and then just stared at the photo for a few seconds, he then turned and looked at Rafael and almost shouted, "When was this taken?"

Rafael looked at the picture a bit mystified, "Three weeks ago sir give or take a day or two, why do you know Sergeant O'Donnell?"

He still stared at the picture for a moment and then looked over at Rafael, "I knew him as a Navy Seal, and he saved my life when I was a young Marine, I was pretty green back then." Joe turned and looked at Adam, "We need to call the Vice President and tell him that Sergeant John O'Donnell is alive!" He then addressed Lang and Angella, "I was told he died close to seven years ago somewhere near here."

Angella moved over next to Joe and then looked over at the Ambassador, "This man is one of main people on the video's I want you to see, but all they call him on the video's is Sergeant."

Adam moved over closers to Joe, he wanted to "Why the Vice President? Why not the President?"

Joe surveyed everyone in the room and then answered Adam, "The Vice President was with me and a few others and a Navy Sea Team saved us after our plane crushed, but then all we knew him by was his code name, Juicy Fruit. Then about seven years ago I found out from one of the men who they all were."

Angella looked at Joe and then at Adam, "I need to get back to the President Palace, if I stay here too long someone might start talking and we cannot have the guards at the camp get word that something is up."

Joe nodding his head as he walked over to Angella, "It might be a good idea if you took one of our radio's and one of our embassy staff with you so we can coordinate and get updates." He turned and looking at Adam, "What do you say Ambassador?"

Adam just nodded they watched one of the videos their mouths gaping, they were stunned, Adam looked over at Joe; "Send Sergeant Samarth Black with you she is a good communications officer."

Adam walked up to Angella, "Can you wait until we can call the President so you can bring her up to speed. We need to start sending these videos and pictures. It should not take more then an hour. We will let it slip that you are having dinner here just in case someone asks why you were here so long."

Angella agreed and sat down on a chair, she knew it was going to be a very long day or two.

CHAPTER 11

Meanwhile back in Washington D.C. Vice President Sam Cook was on his way to give a speech, he felt like he was back on the campaign trail, but he kept reminding himself that it was just a speech to raise money for his party. The next election was coming up soon and he was leaving his position and going back to teaching at West Point the job he adored, being in the spotlight was over as far as he was concerned. Suddenly from his office on of his secret service agents picked up the phone that was ringing, and looked over at Sam with an enigmatic look. "Do you know someone named

Sergeant Joe Pederson? He said that someone
called Juicy Fruit is alive and needs your help?"

Sam jumped out of his seat and grabbed the
phone out of the agent's hand to talk to Joe, "What
do you need, where is he?" Everyone in the office
saw him start to breathing heavier and he turned
white as a ghost as his listened to Joe on the phone
explain the situation. Then the agent just heard
him say, "Call me back in one hour, I had a speech to
make that I need cancel, I will be able to talk more
then and send me all of the pictures and video's you
have!" Sam then handed the phone back to the
agent, sat back down and looked at his agents,
"Inform the driver that I do not need the car, inform
the caucus that the speech will have to wait, and
call the President I need to have an emergency
meeting with her and all of the military staff as
soon as possible!"

"What do you want to tell the people at the fund
raiser?"

"I just came down with the flu!" This was more
important, he only hoped that they could get them
the help they needed fast enough to save everyone
at the camp, including his old friend.

President Betty Jones was enjoying her free
hour that she had set aside to relax and do some
painting. It also gave her time to reflect her job and
how glad she was that she had only two years left.
Time and time again she cursed those two idiots for
getting caught in that sex scandal two months

before the Presidential election. Her party came to her and pleaded with her to run until they found someone else, they never thought she would win, and then she could go back to teaching at Harvard. But she went and got herself elected, damn. The others went to jail and she became the President, which put her life on hold for four years, now fun. She looked over at her cat Fluffy who was sleeping on the rug in middle the oval office, and then she turned back toward her canvas, and started to paint again and sighted. Suddenly her top aide Ann came running her the oval office almost out of breath, "Madame, the Vice President is in his office he wants to meet with you and all of the joint chiefs of staff right away, he said it was an emergency! There apparently are videos and picture he needs everyone to see, something about an American's being imprisoned and one is a military officer, and they need your help. He is just pulling together details right now Madame! He wants to meet you in the war room as soon as possible."

Betty set her paintbrush down and got up removed her smock, and then she headed for the war room. Whatever the hell was going on, she had a feeling was going to be overwhelming and that scared her more then winning that damn election two years ago.

She spotted Sam and his aide almost running toward the war room, one of his secretariats Patty came out distraught with her hand held over her month, heading toward the women's bathroom. As she and Sam were just about to enter she spotted Jill on her knees holding a wastebasket to her face, apparently this was worse than she thought.

Sam and Betty sat down to watch the screen and the first thing they saw was a young girl holding a severed head in her hands.

Betty's face turned ghost white she wanted to pass out, but Sam nudged at her to distract her a bit.

Jill by that time had quit watching the screen and concentrated on other things happening around her but she was still really pale, she heard the fax machine and retrieved the information, "We received some pictures on the fax machine, alone with the video's that were sent. There are five video's attached, we just opened the first one and saw a young lady getting murdered! The information came in was about Senator Barbara Thomas and top military aide Jim Brown."

Sam turned to Jill and motioned her to give him the fax and started to review some of the pictures suddenly he looked shocked and could not believe what he saw, he handed them to Betty for confirmation.

Betty started looking though the pictures and her eyes got huge, she looked back at Sam and nodded, "They said her ship sank three years ago while she was working for the United Nations."

Betty stood up and looked around the room, "Okay everyone, we need solutions get everyone you need on the horn, Ann, get me the numbers of every Admiral and General that is still in town I need to get them here immediately!" Not waiting for anyone to respond she went into a side office out of view, she need to gather her composure; she was concerned and even fought back a tear. She quickly said a short prayer to herself hoping that she was about to do the right thing. Ann came in and gave her the information she had asked for and she started to make calls that would change everything.

Sam looked at Jill as Patty reentered the room, she was still white as a ghost, he helped her into a seat and looked at both of his secretaries, "This is extremely sensitive material, you can't talk about what you have seen here today with anyone outside of this room, hundreds of lives are at stake." He headed off toward a side room to make some calls, "Jill, be sure to let me know if any calls come in for me and I will tell you if I must be interrupted." He then pulled off his tie and entered the side room and prayed that they would not be too late.

Betty entered back into the war room, she observed the staff as they all stood up and looked at her anticipated what she was about to say, It was almost Independence day, so there was just a small stuff present; most had left for the holiday. One of the Admirals was standing with his back to everyone; he was looking at the pictures that were received earlier. He then turned around and headed straight toward Betty, he was almost shaking as he held one of the photos in his hand.

He approached Betty and introduced himself, Admiral James Bender, "Madame President, this photo is my brother-in-law; he was reported deceased seven years ago. Where is he and do you know who this little girl is standing next to him?"

The door opened and Sam hurriedly ran right up to James, "He alive and is being held in a prison camp in Enceladus. We need to get a rescue plan together as soon possible; this mission will be top secret. I heard from my friend who is aiding the new President of Enceladus that this mission had to be done quickly and quietly or lives will be lost."

About then Angella's face appeared on a monitor inside the war room, an agent motioned for the President to come and look at the monitor, she looked exhausted and unsettled, "Can you see me?"

Betty asked the agent to put her on the big screen, "Yes, we can see you, can I ask who you are?"

She gave a broad smile, "I'm Angella Romani, acting President of Enceladus and I am sure you are aware of the situation, and I need your help Madame President. Did you get a chance to review the information that was sent? There are over 400 people being held in a prison camp here, and yes some are Americans we have maybe a day or two at the most to save them, if the guards at the camp find out that President Chavez is dead, we think they will kill all of the prisoners and flee the area."

Admiral Bender walked up to the screen and addressed the President, he held the picture up to the screen so she could see it, "This is my brother-in-law, and do you have any idea when this picture was taken?"

Her face turned from concerned to sorrow, "That picture was taken two months ago after a couple of Marine five star Generals murder my little sister! That little girl is your brother-in-law's daughter and my niece, her name is Janet lightfoot O'Donnell." A lot has happen in that camp, things that are unspeakable, believe me when I tell you that she was born not by choice but is loved. I guess that means we are related Admiral." He slowly lowered the picture with a look of disbelief on his face, then he looked at everyone in the room, "Betty, there is no such thing as a five star general in the Marines."

Angella looked over her shoulder to address and aide and nodded her head yes, then she turned back to the monitor, "I have to get back to the Presidential Palace, if I spend to much time here someone may start talking and the guards may hear about it and that would not be good, we are not sure who we can trust at the moment. The ambassador Flannigan has some of his Marines putting satellite communication equipment into my car, so I can keep in contact with you better at the Presidential Palace Madame President and the rest of your staff."

Betty nodded her head yes as she turned toward James, "Find out what assets we have in the area and how quickly it can get into position!" She then addressed the Vice-President, "Call the congressional leadership and have them in session within the hour. Do not tell them any details yet, for once they will not tell me I acted too slow."

Admiral Bender, headed over to the world map, without saying a word and started to key in information, he needed to keep busy because he started to feel sick to his stomach. Well his wife would be pissed when he had to tell her that they would not be heading to the lake this year. He took a quick look down at a phone, and then shook his head no a few times he couldn't call Margie yet until he had all of his facts, and then go from the President to do so, but he was tempted. From behind him he heard Sam and he seems to be a little excited. "I see that the aircraft carrier U.S.S. Nokomis and its task force X Ray, might be the closed ship to Enceladus and I know her admiral very will. If you would like I will put in a call to him. He was with me when this Sergeant of your was in the Navy as a Seal and that Sergeant saved our bacon and a few others."

Admiral Bender turned and looked at Sam, "Make the call and have him turn toward Enceladus as full steam." Before Sam could turn away, Bender put his right hand on Sam's shoulder, "My nephew is on the Nokomis as a Marine Lieutenant." Bender then turned and walked back toward the President and Vice President who were busy watching some of the videos that were received and both looked pale. He stood at attraction and addressed the President, "I have given this operation the code name Thor's hammer? Sergeant John O'Donnell is a student of ancient Roman and Greek history and he would get a good laugh at this code name." They both agreed and nodded their heads and returned to watching the videos, he turned and headed back toward the chiefs to devise a plan of attack. Suddenly he felt a cold draft for a few second then warmth again, and hoped he wasn't going into shock.

Back at the computer he started to checkup on a few things so he could brief everyone on the operation when his cell phone started to vibrate in his pocket, he took it out and just stared at the number in disbelief. He hesitated for a second and then answered, "Good afternoon, what can I do for you?" He listened to the voice on the other end and his heart started to beat faster, and then he said in an angry voice, "PUT YOUR MOTHER ON!" He looked around the room to see if anyone had heard him.

CHAPTER 12

Admiral Ben Mahoney of the U.S.S. Nokomis was in his cabin removing his shoes getting ready for bed, it had been a long day and he had just started planning for his retirement in a couple weeks. He had a ritual of drinking a warm glass of milk before bed, but before he could drink it the phone rang. "Admiral we have transmission of classified messages under emergency conditions calling for a code RED." The Admiral headed for the COM immediately and without his shoes.

Captain Loren Ross took inventory of the bridge and the crew.

They were all on alert waiting for instructions and nervous they knew that they could be heading to war. Within seconds Admiral Mahoney was on the bridge and he went straight to the radio room without stopping to talk to anyone. Captain Ross took a few steps toward the radio room and paused as he watched the Admiral listen to the incoming message, he noticed the Admiral was disturbed by what he had heard but also exuded confidence.

Commander Bill Hill walked up next to the Captain; "I have the feeling I'm going to miss my son's tenth's birthday next week."

They both watched as the admiral left the radio room and headed right over to the navigation computer and started to input a new heading. Then he looked up and shouted, "Helm you have a new course, flank speed!" "Aye Admiral flank speed ahead."

Bill and Loren both looked at each other startled and Loren slowly walked up to Ben, "What is our heading?"

He looked down at the computer screen for a moment and all he could say was, "HELL!" The Admiral picked up the microphone next to the computer and addressed the crew. "Red alerts all hands to battle stations. This is not a drill, our heading is top secret, and no outside communication will be allowed at this time to ensure our safety and the safety of others." We are on a rescue mission to save over 400 men women and child." The he started to read off names coming in on the computer secure, the last name he read off was Lieutenant John O'Donnell Jr.

He then instructed all chief officers to report to the Operations room. He went over to the communications officer, "We have some video's and pictures coming in on a secure line, I want them sent to the Operations room at once." He then went to operations, once there he saw that the printer was starting to receive some pictures, he grabbed the first one and just stared at it for a few seconds and then grabbed the rest of them, you could see on his face that he was definitely disturbed at what he saw and on of the pictures was of the Admiral's missing daughter, Diane Mahoney. Without a saying a word he headed to the table and sat down at the computer getting ready to look at the videos received, and prepare the mission.

Everyone on the bridge knew something big was about to happen. Captain Ross prepared the crew for the mission.

Lieutenant John O'Donnell Jr. was down in the recreation hall on his laptop looking at some baby furniture, his wife was expecting their first baby next month. He then closed his laptop and stood up ready to report to Operations. He looked around at his men and they all looked a bit shaken they all looked forward to being on liberty once they got back to Miami next week. Some of his men took a step closer to him because they had concerns, but he waved them away and headed out of the recreation hall. He tucked his laptop under his arm and headed toward Operations.

Lieutenant John O'Donnell Jr. Walked into the Operations room, all the high-ranking officers on the ship and they there, and they were all standing around talking quietly voices. O'Donnell felt out of place because he was the youngest ranking officer on the ship he set his stuff on the table in the middle of the room and waited for the Admiral to walk in.

When the Admiral walked into the room everyone stood at attention and saluted, until the Admiral returned the salute and told everyone to have seat.

The Admiral looked the officers over and then looked right at Lieutenant O' Donnell, "Lieutenant remember when you first came on board I told you that your father saved my life many years ago?"

John answered, "Yes, Sir."

The Admiral just stared at John for about ten seconds, "We are about to return the favor, juicy fruit is alive and we are going to save him and those who are imprisoned with him!"

John could not believe what he had just heard, and just stared straight at the Admiral, "Sir, I will have my men ready to jump in ten minutes or less! Just tell me when and where.

"Settle down Lieutenant until we are done here, you do not want to get the prisoners or your men killed jumping into something you are not ready for!" He then looked at the rest of the officers, "This is an air recue mission, and it is the only safe way in. There are over 400 lives at this camp we are heading for and many of them are very young, who will be dead if we do not get them out of the camp, quickly, safely and quietly." He looked down at the Ship's head doctor, "Are your doctors and nurses prepared for casualties, and people who are starving or sick?"

Doctor Henry Cook replied, "Sir, I would have to check but we will be by the time we need to be."

The Admiral took a deep breath, "Then I will see about getting us some help and supplies, in the meantime get sickbay ready for a lot of sick or hurt people. We have about 36 hours before we are ready to lunch our recue mission so I want every officer to get your teams ready for the worst, I have maps, videos and photos of the camp. There will be another briefing in Oh three hundred hours so get your teams ready." The Admiral pulled aside Lieutenant O'Donnell Jr., "I have a few more things to tell you before you leave to get your men ready." He then addressed his Major, "Major Morgan, I have a map of the camp to help you start plan."

Major Ann Morgan stood up at attention and gave a glance John's way and responded to the Admiral, "Sir, I will have it ready for you in less then oh ten hundred hours, all I need to know is the schematics to calculate how many helicopter and Marines I will have to use."

The Admiral acknowledged the Major, "Right now we have five birds on board, but let me know what you need and I will accommodate you, I can make a few requests, the most important thing is we need to get them all out fast and safely."

After specking to the Admiral, Lieutenant O'Donnell walked back into the room where all of his men were awaiting orders. They all stood up at attention and saluted O'Donnell responded and ordered them at ease, some men went back to playing cards. Everyone can see that Lieutenant O'Donnell was under extreme stress and about to explode, he walked up to the table, grabbed and flipped it over. Everyone in the room jumped up, they had never seen him this mad before.

He looked at his men and saw that his cousins, who were Navy Seals, had entered the room as well. "I need volunteers for a recue mission to save the lives of men, women and children being held captive!" Then he looked at his cousin Little Bear, and addressed them all, "One of the prisoners is a U.S. Marine and before he became a Marine he was a Navy Seal for close to 17 years!"

Little Bear's eyes were fixated toward O'Donnell, "Only one man has every done that and that man was your father!"

Lieutenant O'Donnell just nodded his head, "I also have a young sister there too."

CHAPTER 13

Margie eyes sprang open from a restless sleep when she heard her daughter Susan's death defying screams coming from her room down the hallway. She grabbing her pistol off the nightstand jumped out of bed and ran toward Susan room, her pistol all set and ready to confront whomever maybe in Susan's room. But when she entered she never expected to see a headless ghostly figure standing in front of Susan's bed and before she could move it disappeared. She moved toward the front of the bed looking around the room a little stunned not comprehending what she had seen. She then went over to the window and looked outside, there was nothing there. She went over to Susan who looked terrified and was a bit in shock. She was sitting up in her bed and white as a ghost.

Margie comforted her but kept her pistol on hand just in case, "What was that?"

She tear up, "That was Mary, Janet's mother!"

She head her close, "Who is Mary and who is Janet?"

She slowly looked up at her mother, "Janet is my little sister, that Mary was her mother.

Margie sat down on Susan's bed, but still looking toward in the direction of what she had seen, then she looked at Susan with sadness in her eyes, "I know that I said that I would not have your father declared dead until I had his remains, but it has been over seven years and he is still missing.

Everyone said he died when he fall off of that cliff seven years ago."

Susan turned and looked up at her mother, "He is not dead mom, and wherever he is, he has suffered greatly, and now I have a sister. The Marines and the Navy are going to get him! Call uncle James and ask him about Thor hammer, it the code name they are using to go and get daddy!"

Margie looked down at the pistol still in her hands and then at Susan, "Your uncle is probably half way to the family cabin, you know his family gets to use it this July 4th weekend."

Susan reached over and took the phone off of her nightstand and ran out of her bedroom and into the bathroom across the hall.

Margie didn't know what to think and just shook her head as she walked up to the closed bathroom door and tried to open it, but it was locked. She reached up to her red hair and pulled out a bobby pin, "Open this door this minute or I will open it and I will take away your phone and TV privileges for a week, young lady."

Just as Margie was about to stick the pin into the lock Susan opened the door with tears falling down her face, she handed the phone to her mother, "Uncle James want to talk to you and he is not happy!"

She was somewhat annoyed at this point and took the phone answering with that mother tone Susan was very familiar with. "Listen little brother, I'm sorry but." Was all the farther she got.

She heard her brother James and he was shall we say, just pissed, "I do not know how you found out about this operation so fast, but do not even mention that code name on a unsecured phone line again, do you hear me big sister! There are a few hundred live at stake if word gets out about his operation. Are both of you at home?"

Margie looked at the phone for about five second, not sure how to respond to that, "Yes we are at home, why do you ask?"

"I'm going to send a car to pick you two up and you will need to pack for at least a few days." Not another word from James came out as she heard the line go dead.

She looked at the phone in her hand for a second, "Susan, go and pack some clothes for at least few days and do not talk about this until we get to your uncle James."

Susan turned and ran into her room, but stopped just shy of it then turned and looked up at her mother, "Mom, pack your uniform too I have the feeling you are going to need it."

Margie started to walk to her bedroom and sat the phone down on a table in the hallway; she could not believe what was going on.

One hour later Margie was setting her suitcase down next to the front door. She looked out of the window and saw Paul Blue heading home from his early morning run. She heard a commotion and looked over her shoulder she saw Susan carrying her suitcase that looked way too full, but that was okay, she knew her daughter too well. Margie took deep breath, and looked back outside. She understood that Paul moved next to her after John went miss, to help her if she needed it, after he had retired and opened a restaurant with two of his Navy Seal buddies. She Picking up her house key and then opened the desk next to the front door and took something out of the top drawer and headed out carrying her suitcase and garment bag. Susan tagged alone dragging her suitcase as well.

Paul was at the end of his early morning jog when he spotted Margie and Susan setting down their suitcase at the end of the driveway. He watched Margie start to walk toward him and the look on her face was the look he was all too familiar with. Sorrow and fear all at the same time and disbelief.

Margie walked up to Paul and held out her left hand, "We will be gone for a few days and we cannot tell you where we are going or why. Will you bring in our mail and paper while we are gone?"

Paul stuck out his hand and took the other item she was holding as well, without looking at it and watched a car pulling up to the end of Margie's driveway. An Army private got out and open the truck to load the luggage and then opened the door for Susan to get in.

Margie reached out with her other hand and cover his hands, completely, "Never forget." She then turned and walked over to the car, wiping another tear shed that she had been fighting to conceal.

Paul looked down to look at what was in his hand finally and looked back up quickly as he saw the car pull away and then back down at his hand again. He closed his hand he headed into his house, he had to make plans and call his old Navy seal buddies to meet. Planning could not be done over the phone but he needed to show them what Margie had put in his hand and someone was going to pay big time for not telling the truth about Big John if he had anything to say about it.

CHAPTER 14

One hour later Paul pulled his car into his restaurant called HOMEPORT and he saw that both of his buddies were already there so he just walked in and over to a table where they were waiting. Jimmy Johnson was the head cook and he loved to cook for his friends, so of course there was a lot of food and drink for this sit down, and they probably would need it. But you never want to make him mad he was well over two hundred and that was pure muscle. Sam Blue was a happy go lucky guy, people loved his personality, but just like Jimmy he was not a man you wanted mad at you either, he was not as buff but still all muscle and agile, he was a quick son of a gun.

Jimmy reached out and poured Paul a cup of coffee and then looked up at Paul, "Ok, why did you get us up this early in the morning?"

Paul sat down, and gave the shut up signal he then reached into his shirt pocket and throw down the item Margie had giving him, "Margie gave that to me just before she and Susan got picked up by the army and she told me to never forget!"

Jimmy slowly reached out and picked up the stick of juicy fruit gum and then looked at both Paul and Sam, "He's alive! Those two bastards have been lying too her about John being dead, all these year and trying to put her out of business!"

Sam slamming his fists down so hard onto the table he almost broke it, "The next time they come here to eat, I will not serve them, if I do not kill them first!"

Paul gestured for them to calm down, then he picked up his coffee cup and took a snip, "Lets not go off half crocked here. I have the feeling the Government would not want us to jeopardize anyone's life at the moment, and I'm sure as hell do not want to get Margie mad at me."

Both Sam and Jimmy both laugh then Jimmy gave Sam a little shove, "I would rather face a thousand angry Taliban in my underwear then get Margie mad at me. You know want they say about those redheads when then get mad. They are like a small stick of dynamite, with a very short fuse."

Jimmy just shook his head, "John was the only one who could ever handle that redhead."

Just then Dawn walked out of the kitchen and stand down next to Jimmy and put her hand on top of her husband's, "All I know is that without her help, we could have never bought this restaurant a few years ago. Last year she even helped us make payroll after we had that kitchen fire that was arson and the insurance coverage just wasn't enough and she never asked for any return!"

Sam looked over at Dawn and then at Paul, "I still say it was those two brothers who were trying to buy us out that started that fire. The fire started just after we turn down their offer, although we can't prove it!"

Paul looked down at his hands, "They also have been making a move on Margie's business too. They want to expand, so they say."

Dawn looked around the table, "I would love to find out where all that money they have had come from, they sure have been spending a lot on fast cars and other stuff these last few years?"

Sam nodded his head yes, "From what I've heard, it is has been all cash too."

Sam looked down at his cup of coffee, "All of the money Margie had and some of her dad's went into that construction of the businesses down in Miami two years ago."

CHAPTER 15

While the meeting was taking place back at the restaurant, Margie and Susan's car pulled up to the back door of the White House, they were met by her Brother Admiral Bender who was accompanied by two Marine as well, he was not happy. He opened the door to the car and helped them both out of the car, then address the Marines, "Get they suitcase and take them into the room they have been assigned here." He heard a yes Admiral sir and then faced Margie and Susan, he got down on one knee so he would be on the same level as his niece, "I have some very important people who would like to talk to you Susan about the information you received about your dad being alive. Do not talk to anyone until I tell you to okay? There are a lot of lives a stake, not only your dad's, he is with others."

Susan turned and looked up at her mother who was overwhelmed at the moment just looking at the White House. Then she looked back at her Uncle, "I think I understand, Uncle, I want to help any way I can."

Admiral Bender stood back up, he reached out took Susan by the hand and led her into the White House with Margie in tow. Margie still could not believe she was in the White House and that John was still alive after all of these years even though she suspected it. Once inside, Margie grabbed her brother's elbow angrily. "Where is he? What happened to him?"

Looking down at his elbow then at Margie then gave her a little smile, "I will fill you both in once we are down in the briefing room and not before."

Ten minutes later Margie was sitting at a table looking at some picture, she raised her hand to wipe a tear off of her face as she looked up at her brother. "How could this have happed to him?"

James just shook his head, "I'm not sure as we are still getting informant about what is going on down there, but it looks like he may have been betrayed by those two Lieutenants in this picture." He handed Margie a picture of two men dressed in Marine uniform.

Margie's eyes got huge as she looked at the picture, "I know both of these guys, and one is trying to put me out of business! The other one works for a U.S Senator, they are both not good men, they both seem to have a lot of money these days."

James just took a deep breath, "From what I have read so far, they maybe in the drug business and a few other things, like money laundering. John and those two were on the same ship, when he went missing a few years ago." He took a deep breath before continuing, "We have just sent some NCIS agents to keep an eye on them until we are ready to begin the raid, we do not want them to know we are onto them and have them tip our hand.

Margie was trying to control her temper as she again went through the pictures, "I want to be there when they are when everything goes down, I have earned that right after all of these years thinking he was dead. By the way what they did to Janet's mother! You have my word I will not get in the way of the operation only if I have to defend myself!"

James just looked at Margie, he knew when not to argue with her, "I will see what I can do, but I cannot make any promises." Just then one of he aids handing him piece of paper, he studied it and then handed it to Margie, once she has read it, she was infuriated, she held the piece of paper in her hands almost shaking, "I'll kill them for this!" She stood up abruptly and marched around the table for a few seconds and then sat back down, "John knew I did not drink, he hated being around those who drank too much, in fact his bourdon of chose was ice tea when we went out, even on our wedding night, his buddies would make a jokes about it."

James put his hand on top of Margie's, "John Jr. is on the U.S.S. Nokomis and I will make sure he tells John that you and the kids did not die in a car wreck after a night of heavy drinking a year after he went missing, if he knew you don't drink I don't think he would believe it anyway, he probably knew it was a scheme to make him more cooperative."

CHAPTER 16

Admiral Mahoney was on the bridge on the phone with Admiral Dwyer, "I'm going to need some more doctors and nurse with Pediatric training if this goes to hell, we only have one or two here right now."

Dwyer looking at the phone in his hand with a heavy heart, "I will find you as many Doctors and Nurse with Pediatric training as fast as I can. Is there any thing ease you need Admiral?"

Mahoney paused for a moment in thought; "I could use a few more helicopter we have only five that are in service right now. It might be a good idea to get the hospital ship U.S.S. Mercy to head toward us too just in case we do assume we will end up with sick and injured people, regardless. My little brother Gregory Mahoney is her Captain"

"I will get you want you need, and have as many ship as I can be moving toward you within hour." Dwyer responded as he was writing down the information.

Down in sickbay Doctor Cook Walked up to his head nurse, "I need you to get everyone to their cabin that are able to continue their care and recovery there because we might need every bed and setup all the beds for triage." He then whistled to get everyone's attention to hear what he was about to say; "You should have seen Lieutenant O'Donnell jump when he was told Juicy fruit was alive."

From one of the beds nearby they all heard a gravely Brooklyn voice, "Did you say that Juicy fruit is alive?"

Doctor Cook looked over at Lieutenant Amy Becker who had just had her appendix token out; she was astonished and climbing out of bed. "Lieutenant let me get someone to help you to get to your cabin."

Lieutenant Becker now with a heavy Spanish accent grabbed a knife off of the food tray next to her bed, "Get out of my way, I need to talk with the Admiral first." What follow was a rambling in Spanish as she walked out of sickbay.

Doctor Cook looked at his nurse quite surprised "My Spanish is a little rusty, but did she just tell me that my mother wore size 11 combat boots to bed?"

The nurse just looked at him, "I did not even now she spoke Spanish, but yes that was close enough."

Doctor cook walked over to the COM, "I had better warn the Admiral that Lieutenant Becker is heading his way why with a knife and very pissed off!"

Lieutenant Becker slowly make her way toward the bridge and was confrontational as she neared the bridge she saw the Admiral standing in front of her with his arms crossed. "Lieutenant Becker drop the knife and go back to sickbay or your cabin right now that is an order!"

Lieutenant Becker dropped the knife and tried to stand at attention and saluted and with her Brooklyn voice, "Admiral, you remember when I came on board I said that we had met before?"

"Yes, I remember that you also told me that if you ever figured out where we had met, you would have to put a bullet between my eyes!" He answers as two Marines moved up behind Lieutenant Becker ready to grab her if the Admiral gave the word.

Looking over her shoulder at the two Marines she held her right hand out and in broken Spanish she said, "Mister Navy person can I have my favored hand grenade back? Or do I have the Navy Seals that are standing behind you shot you? I will fly on his mission because I own him everything, Admiral, just like you do!"

Admiral Flannigan's eye got bigger and his heart heavier as his memory took him back to that day, he took one step toward her, "You will fly on this mission, and you have my word on that! Now get to your cabin and I will let you know when the next briefing is Lieutenant."

Lieutenant Becker nodded but did not move, "I have one more person I need to talk to first, Sir."

Admiral Flannigan looked at one of the Marines, after the Lieutenant has talked to Master Sergeant Robert Bowden, make sure she makes it back to her cabin!" "Yes, Admiral."

One of the Marines held out his arm to help the Lieutenant as she turned to leave the Admiral and from behind him he heard the Captain, "What was that all about?"

Without turning around to answer the Captain, "If I was to tell you about it I would have to put a bullet between your eye it's still classified the last time I checked Captain."

Master Sergeant Robert Bowden was working on a 50-caliber machine gun on one of the CH-53E Super Stallion helicopter with his son he was also a Marine Sergeant. He stopped when he spotted Lieutenant Becker heading his way with the help of another Marine Lance Corporal. He wiped his hand on a rag and stood up and waited for her, he knew she just had surgery and was not up to snuff yet.

Lieutenant Becker walked up to Bowden and stood up as straight as her body allow and they both saluted each other, "Sergeant I have two things I need you to do for me, first can you find some red paint and under my name on my helicopter write Death before dishonor! Second when we return to Miami, I want your granddaughter to meet us at the pier wearing the scarf I put on your leg 18 years ago if she still has it."

Master Sergeant Bowden just stared at Lieutenant Becker for a moment he could not believe what he had just heard and then gave her a large smile, "I will personal paint it on your ship and as for your scarf, I could never get rid of it. I will make sure she is wearing it and on the pier to greet you, she has always wanted to meet you and thank you for saving my live."

Lieutenant Becker turned and with aide headed to her cabin to get ready for the mission.

Bowden just watches as Becker left the area and then spotted a navy chief, "Chief, I need some red paint and a brush, the redder the better!"

From behind him he heard his son, "What hell was that all about?"

He turned to his son and smiled, "All I can say is that your little sister and brother would not be here without her help and the Navy Seal's she was with back 18 years ago." He couldn't believe how much she had changed over the last 18 years, from a scared fifteen-year-old teenager to a proud Marine Osprey helicopter pilot.

CHAPTER 17

In a Navy hospital near Miami, doctor Lieutenant Sandy "O'Donnell was going over some medical files on children that had came in the hospital today, when one of the nurses at the station looked past Sandy, "Doctor, an Admiral heading this way and he looks hurried."

Sandy turned and spotted the Admiral heading straight for her and you could see the sense of urgency in his pace. He was carrying large envelope in his right hand.

Admiral Ken Gibbs stopped right in front of Sandy as she saluted and he handed her the envelope, "Doctor you are being reassigned, your orders are in this envelope and you are not to open it until you are in the car that is waiting outside for you."

Sandy looked at the envelope that said TOP SECERT on it and then back up at the Admiral, "Well this is a shock I am being reassigned and I just started here two days ago?"

The Admiral just grinned, "Well, congratulations and welcome to being in the service, all I was told to do was get a car for you and give you that envelope." Then he got in close and whispered and to her, "Juicy fruit is alive."

Without a word she grabbed her go bag from her office and all but ran toward the exit, she could not believe that her dad was still alive. Once outside she jumped into the back seat of the car and started to rip open the envelope, just as the car started to move. She pulled out a picture and her eyes got huge, she was shocked at what she had just seen. Then she took out the formal correspondence and just shook her head in disbelief what she read was disturbing and a tear started to fall down her face.

Doctor Ben Smith and his wife Jill who was a nurse were on their way out for dinner and the Opera, this was their first day off in two weeks. But, just as they were getting into the car, Ben heard his cell phone ring and he reached into his pocket to answers it with a frown. He saw the number calling, and looked up at his wife, "It's the Navy."

Jill put both of her hands on top of their car and buried her head between them, "No, we just finish our tour three weeks ago."

Ben answered his phone and turned toward his wife, "We are both being called in and they want us to head right to the air force base now

Ben and Jill still had their go bags in the car just in case. Jill got into the car and slammed the door and looked at her husband wanting some sort of answer, "Some high ranking officer's kid had better break something!" Then she crossed her arms as they headed out.

Later they pulled into the air force base and showed the guards their IDs they were directed to a parking space off to the side, "Park your car over there and the jeep will take you to the hanger for a briefing with the others." He then stood up and gave them both a salute and watched them park, he wondered what is going on, it had never been this busy and this made the fourth doctor and sixth nurse to come in tonight, but it was obviously above his pay grade.

They got out grabbed their go bags and headed to the jeep with three other passengers another pediatric doctor and two pediatric nurses. Ben looked at his wife, "Whatever is going on it must be big!"

Once they were in the jeep the driver took off rapidly to a hanger with seven Ospreys, motors running and two apache helicopters that looked heavily armed. They both spotted Doctor Sandy O'Donnell who they knew and they saw that she had been crying so they walked up to her.

Sandy saw them wiped a tear off her face and moved toward them and just hugged Jill, "I'm glad they have called the best pediatrics they could for this."

Jill looked at Sandy, "Do you know what is going on here?"

Sandy nodded her head yes, "It's about my dad, he is alive along with a lot of kids and they are in a prison camp called Camp Hell!"

Just then a Marine Brigade General Artie Goodman, walked into the hanger followed by a female aide and waved for everyone to get closer. He looked over all of the doctors and nurses and started briefing them, "I'm sorry to ruin your Forth of July weekend, but there are over 400 lives that need your help and many of them are young children. We will be flown out to the U.S.S. Nokomis and then to hospital ship U.S.S. Mercy, but the Mercy may not get there in time for this recue operation so first you will be taken to the U.S.S. Nokomis." He took a deep breath and continued, "This is a classified operation, and if things go bad you need to be ready, there will be no communication too many lives are at stake. We need to get out and onto the waiting helicopters and get moving; we will stop and be refueled twice on our way to the Nokomis. We will be arriving at the Nokomis sometime after sunset if all goes as planned, get some sleep while we are in the air, you might need it. You will be transported to the U.S.S. Mercy, if she gets there on time." He then headed toward the exit with his aide in tow at a quick pace.

Sandy caught him before he boarded and showed him the picture of her father and Janet, "Can you explain this to me?"

Artie looked at the picture and then at Sandy, "Fly with me, once we are in the air, I will tell you everything I know about this."

Just then a female with a camera in her hand came running into the hanger flashing her pass, "Hi, I'm Patty Brown, I work for CCN and I received a call about needing a pool reporter for whatever is going on. Can anyone tell me what this is all about?"

Artie pointed to his aide, "Lieutenant Candace Lager will fill you in once we are in the air."

Patty snapped a few photos around the hanger and then joined the rest heading toward the helicopters, she was anxious to find out what was going on call she got was mysterious in natures which of course fueled her curiosity, the call said come here at once to be a pool reporter and not to tell anyone. She wished she had the time to call her husband so he would not worry about her, but what she didn't know was he had been informed already.

Just as the last of them are getting onto the helicopters a jeep pulled up and an old Navy Doctor got off of it, and hurried on   Artie got off of his helicopter and helped him get on board and shook his hand, "I had the feeling you would be showing up. Doctor."

Doctor Dale Thompson returned Artie's handshake and accepted his help as he climbed aboard, "I may not be able to do surgery, but I can still work a triage unit damn it, and just like you I owe juicy fruit everything I have become today."

CHAPTER 18

Admiral Mahoney walked onto to the bridge, everyone saluted then he walked up to Captain Ross, "Any word on the drones that were launched three hours ago from the base at Enceladus?"

Captain Ross turned and gave Mahoney a smile; "They should be over the camp within the hour Admiral.

Ross pulled the Admiral aside, "We just got some more information on your friend who is being held there and you may or may not want to share it with his son!   We also received a list of all of the doctors and nurses who are on their way here, the officers and Marines who are coming too."

Then he looked the other communication and threw out a few swear words under his breath then he read it a second time before leaving the bridge and going to find Lieutenant O'Donnell, he needed to share what he has just learned. This was going to make him upset and angry and he would not blame him if he wanted to take off right now and beat the crap out of someone.

As he was in the briefing room watching John reading the communication John started slowly swearing under his breath, "I will kill them for this, if my mom doesn't kill them first!" Then he turned and walked over to a map of the camp, "Is there any way we can get word to my dad that we are coming?"

The Admiral put his right hand on John's shoulder, "Not at this time, it's too risky."

John pointed at the picture of one of the building, "Can we drop something though the hole in the roof of the building they are kept in?"

The Admiral looked at the picture and shook his head no, "Not without the guards seeing it first, I'm sorry, but if I know your dad, I would not be surprised that he wouldn't be spoofed by this propaganda." He looked over the picture again and then back at John, "We will have drones over the camp within a the hours, if you want I can have the live feed to you and the rest of your men too that way they can get the layout and know what is going on at the camp."

CHAPTER 19

A day earlier Sergeant John O'Donnell had been working in one of the caves at the archaeology site, digging with just his bare hands to try and find some artifacts. Mostly he and the others just found small bones, but some days when they did find something of value or the archaeologist Ben Black would tell them if it was worth keeping. He liked to think he was Indiana Jones, but to him it was all about the money, not history and he loved having prisoners do all the work for him. He never entered the caves at all, but instead had video cameras set up and a speaker system so he could relate to them where to work. It was harder than working in the poppy fields, it was dark and dirty and the only light they had was, the one on the miner helmets they were given. Crackling over the speaker they were told that it was time to head out and back to camp, John led everyone back to the entrance. Suddenly he realized that Abbie who was about six years old was still busy trying to dig something out of the wall, John went back to the cave to her, "Leave it for the next time Abbie, it's time to leave."

But Abbie was persistent and just kept trying to dig something out of the bottom of the wall she looked over her shoulder at John, "I just need one more minute."

John just shook his head and left the cave and felt a rush of fresh air, suddenly the ground started to shake and you could hear the dirt closing in and a cloud dust came out of the cave. John turned to rush back into the cave, but was stopped by Hallmar who had his pistol drawn jabbing it into John's stomach, grinning ear to ear. "You do not have time to go back in, it will be dark soon unless you do not want to eat today?"

He Looked over Hallmar's shoulder toward the cave and he could barely make out Abbie voice, "Help me!" He then got angry and shouted, "We have to get her out!"

Hallmar pushed John and shoved his gun at John to get into the line, John moved reluctantly toward the rest of the prisoners, "If she is alive next week you can dig her out then!" He then gave John another larger shove this time, "NOW MOVE!" Everyone put their heads down, hauntingly they too could hear Abbie calling.

Marie who had been working one of the artifact sifting screens took a few steps toward him and quietly told him, *"Do something, she will die in there if we do not help her!"*

He was stoned faced and he reached out and urged her toward the others, "I KNOW! So move!" I have to figure something out. He couldn't s look back at the cave, it made him sick to his stomach, he was tired of carrying dead bodies to the fire pit, and there were a lot even children from starvation, sickness, or women dying in childbirth. He tried not to look at Marie, she too was pregnant and he worried, he silently headed back to the camp with everyone deep in thought.

President Angella Romani was standing next to the truck that would be carry the food to the camp today. With her American friends they had put some hidden cameras and microphones with it, and they were clever no one would find them, the driver was the regular who could be trusted. She went up to the driver with a small piece of paper, "If you can get close to the Sergeant give him this piece of paper do it without anyone seeing you, if it is too risky bring it back with you. If anyone asks why you are bringing more food, tell them it is President Chavez's birthday gift."

The driver took the piece of paper and put it in his pocket, "I will do my best madam." Then he got into the truck started it up and heading down the road toward the camp.

Angella watched the truck until it was out of sight then walked over to the American Ambassador Adam Flannigan, "I hope he can get the message to your Sergeant so he knows that help is on the way."

Adam took Angella by the elbow. "Let go over to the tent and watch the monitors to see what happens at the camp, when the truck get there." They both went to a tent that had been set up as base; it was camouflaged and had a full computer system and monitors, both of them watched in anticipation as it neared the camp.

When the prisoners were walking back to camp, John was still thinking about Abbie her voice would never leave his head. Some of the guards have been drinking and some smoking pot they grew themselves. Hallmar and some of the other guards were toting their swords waving them around acting like idiots. Hallmar noticed the truck approaching, John was leery about this food truck, it was different the normal truck with a large door in the back, the driver was the regular driver.

Hallmar staggered up to John holding a bottle in one hand, "In celebration of our President Chavez, he has order some special food and there is enough for everyone to eat tonight. But first I want everyone to line up in front of the truck and sing happy birthday to our President."

John motioned for everyone to form three lines in front of the truck, he kept one eye on the guards who are trying to stand up straight as they sang happy birthday, all of the prisoners sang as well, no one wanted trouble. Once they are done singing and before John and could anything a young girl about six years old named Macall moved toward the back of the truck.

Macall had her hand on the handle of the door when a shout blurted out from Hallmar, "Freeze." He moved in from the side of the truck to behind Macall, staggering, his sword behind his back, "I did not say Simon says." Before John could move, speak or do anything he swung his sword and chopped off her hand. John rushed over and ripped a dirty shirt off of one of the prisoner who still had a decent one left, and wrapped Macall's severed limb to try and stop the bleeding.

Before John can say anything, he heard another young girl scream; it was Hadria shouting at Hallmar like a Marine Drill instructor but in Spanish. Hallmar dropped his bloody sword to his side and approached Hadria backing her up to the side of the truck and then he looked at the other prisoner and shouted, "Where is your twin sister Sabeen?"

Sabeen slowly moved forward from the back of the group and moved up next to her sister. She stood tall and brave, but they both knew they were in trouble. Hallmar backhands Sabeen and then Hadria, not only once then he motioned to one of the guards, "Put them both in the sweatbox until tomorrow evening." Then he looked at the driver of the truck, "Take it back and tell the President want happen here, he will not be happy, none of them will be fed either."

The driver had moved in behind one of the little girl trying to look non-Chelan about the whole matter, and as he started to close up the truck stuck the piece of paper in the back of her pants and very softly said, *"For your sergeant."* She nodded her head yes, then he got back into the truck and drove out of the camp upset at what he had seen and heard.

All of the guards watched the truck pull away to make sure he was not giving any signals to anyone in the camp, but what they didn't know was John had taught the prisoner sign language. As the guards were distracted, the prisoners were upset and wanted to start a fight, John just signed back "Tomorrow morning." Then he picked up Macall and carried her back to the barrack without saying a word.

CHAPTER 20

Lieutenant John O'Donnell's skin crawled as he watched the guard cut off the young girl's hand and backhand the other two girls and send them to that box near the fence line. Just as he was about to go over plans his cousin Little Bear got his attention, "Look at the prisoners hands!"

John moved closer to the monitor and then looked back at his cousin, "are they signing? We have to tell the admiral what is going on at the camp we can't wait another day!" John and his cousin high tailed it to find the Admiral not realizing Navy Corpsman Amy Thomas was just staring at the monitor.

When Amy was a little girl she was with her mother, who was running for congress. They decided to visit a Reservation in AZ that was set up for Soldiers and they even met the chief of the tribe. While her mother was talking to the chief he walked up to Amy and put his hand on her head and looked into her eyes, "What do you what to be when you grow up?"

Amy turned and looked at her father with admiration and answered, "I want to be a Navy Corpsman like my dad was and my grandfather were."

The chief closed his eyes for a moment and then looked up at the sky, when he looked back at her he said, "You may not understand this yet, the spirits tell me that you will be what you inspire to be, and when you are a Navy Corpsman, you must make a jump with the men of the night, it will be after you see she with one hand and the two women in the box. You most tell the men of the night, that your Soldier name is Shamus. You must jump with them no matter what anyone says the great chief told me lives will be in your hands Shamus, and that you must go." Without a word she turned and ran after the Navy Seal's.

CHAPTER 21

Admiral Ben Mahoney was on the bridge watching the same live feed as the Marines on the ship, but he didn't catch the prisoners signing to each other. He grabbed the air rests on his chair firmly, he wanted to fly out of his seat and do something immediately but he also knew that he was hours away yet, from being prepared, he choked trying not to throw up. Under his breath he just whispered help was coming. He was staring at the monitor and something suddenly caught him in disbelief he, spotted his daughter moving the prisoners back into their barracks and like the rest she looked ragged and she may have been beaten.

Lieutenant John O'Donnell Jr. and four Navy Seal came hastily onto the bridge and went over to some pictures of the camp that were on a tractable table. The Seals were looking at the pictures of the prisoner barracks and talking fast amongst themselves. John looked up at the Admiral, "Sir, we need to get someone into the camp the prisoners are going to start a riot in the morning!"

Admiral Mahoney stood up and went over to the team, "Do you know this for certain? Because it would be a one-way trip, for everyone who jumps into that camp tonight, we are not close enough and can't launch our rescue operation until early morning. The U.S.S. Mercy will not be here for at least five hours, and the doctors and nurses should be arriving on board here in a few hours too.

Little Bear looked at his cousins and the Admiral, he held up a certain picture of the barrack, "Sir, if you can get us in quietly we can parachute through this hole in the roof, we will have to have something on us not to alarm the others so they know we are friendlies, they we will make sure they remain calm until help has arrived."

From the doorway Navy Corpsman Amy Thomas appeared, "Permission to join the Seal team, Sir?" She looked directly at Little Bear, "I'm Shamus, the medicine woman you must take me with you."

Admiral Mahoney moved up to the table and addressed the team, "You start making a plan and I will notify President Romani and President Jones of what we have come up with and see if they will agree in this operation."

CHAPTER 22

President Romani was setting in front of the monitors with her head in her hands, she could never unseen what she has just witnessed on the monitors.

Lieutenant Rafael put his hand on her shoulder as he listened to a message coming in and then looked over at Ambassador Flannigan, "The driver manger to get the message to one of the girls, just before he was ordered out.

Before the Ambassador could reply to Rafael communications were coming in from the ship the U.S.S. Nokomis, he told the caller he would get back to them, then he addressed Romani and Rafael. He seated himself next to Romani she just kept looking at one of the monitors, "It looks like we may have to move faster then we have planned. Some of the Navy Seals who were watching the live feed saw some of the prisoners using sign language planning a riot. Sergeant O'Donnell signed back at them that it would start in the morning." Then his gaze went up at Rafael, "The Navy Seal's want to parachute through a hole in the roof of the prisoners building, but they need a distraction tonight."

Romani as if she suddenly awoke from a bad dream looked at Flannigan her eyes red from crying and being exhausted and walked passed Rafael she moved over to a map of the area and pointed at an area about two miles from the camp. Flannigan, "Ask them how much time do they need to get into the building." Rafael, "If we were to blow up these old oil tanks, would they be able to see the explosion from the camp?"

Rafael looked over the map, "It'll be a big one I will make sure they are able to see it. Beside those tank have been leaking for years so it wouldn't be a surprise if they were to blow up, I think there is going to be an electrical problem over there tonight, well isn't that a bummer." Then he snickered

Flannigan grinned and quickly got back on the phone to give the go. Romani looked back at the map with a worried look on her face and then looked at Rafael, "Well, if we are going to do it we might as well give them a little more time, so blowing up the building next to the tanks would give it a bang don't you think? And it would take longer to put out and loud."

Flannigan put his phone down and looked down at the map, "They will need at least five minutes to parachute into the building without being seen. We need to coordinate the jump two hours after sunset."

Rafael looked at his watch and then at Flannigan, "I will start to get things ready, it shouldn't take us too long to set this up at the oil tanks."

Flannigan looked at Romani and then back at Rafael, "It might be a good idea to send some of my Marines to help your men with the explosives."

Romani picked up the phone and called Admiral Mahoney, "Admiral, when I tell them that President Chavez is dead and to surrender and they do not. Tell your Marines to send them all to HELL!"

CHAPTER 23

President Betty Jones was going over some files about the camp after watching all of the videos and she felt sick to her stomach she just could not believe that her good friend congressional Senator Barbara Thomas, who top aide was in the drug business and a rapist. She received an update from Admiral Mahoney about the Navy Seal operation. The door to the war room opened and Margie now was wearing her Navy uniform with the rank of Captain.

Margie looked tired as she entered the war room, "I told Susan to try and get some sleep as it might be a long next few days."

President Jones took Margie over to a table that has a map of the camp on it and pointed at the hole in the roof of the prisoners building. "We just heard from Admiral Mahoney, that a Seal team may parachute through this hole in the roof, shortly after sun down. It looked like the prisoners know how to use sign language and if we do not stop them, they will start a riot in the morning."

Margie just looked down at the picture and then looked at the President, "That is something my husband would have taught them so they could talk over long distant without the guards noticing."

Betty looked at Margie and then put her arm on her shoulder, "I want you to see the video that we took on the truck that was bringing food to the camp. I know that it is awful to watch and I warn you that it is graphic but it will show you why the prisoners want to fight and why the Seals are going in tonight."

Margie watched the video and was silent as she watched her husband's face when he carried the girl into the barrack followed by all of the prisoners, some looking over their shoulders watching as the two twins were put into the sweatbox. They all knew that they would not live very long in the sweatbox with the tropical temperatures.

An aide entered and handed the president a note, she read it and then looked at Margie, "NCIS just found out that the Browns are going to be having breakfast at HOMEPORT in the early morning."

Margie gave the President a little smile, "I know the owners of HOMEPORT and they are good friends they also are former Navy Seals of one of my husband teams. I would like to be there when they are arrested."

President Jones, though for a moment, "They will be at the restaurant about one hour before the recue starts. I will put in a call to NCIS and the FBI and ask about you being there and it will be their call?"

CHAPTER 24

Admiral Mahoney walked into the briefing room where the Navy Seals and Navy Corpsman having been receiving instructions about their jump. They all stood up at attention when he entered the room and he was caring the order that either would be go or no go, "Be seated, Your jump is a go. You will be taking off just after sunset, immediately after the choppers with the doctors and nurses arrive." He then relayed the idea for the distraction, "From the time you jump you will have a little over five minutes to get into the building."

Little Bear stood up, "Sir we will use what we call the ladder to parachute into the building." Looking at Corpsman Thomas, "That way, we will be landing within inches of each other."

Thomas spoke up, "I have made six night jumps and I'm the only one to hit the bull's-eye. I plan on being the third person out of that plane. You guys had better be careful the and not land on top of me!" Pointer her finger at all of the Navy Seals, "I'm not going to argue about it either!"

Little Bear gave her a little laugh, "I would not even think about it, but you might want to carry as much medical supplies as you can, I have the feeling you are going to need as much as you can safely carry."

Two hours later Lieutenant O'Donnell walked up to Charlie Brown and the rest of Seals and the Corpsman was loaded down with medical supplies, they were waiting for the helicopters to land, "I have the feeling my sister is on one of those helicopters and I do remember Charlie, she told you that she would give you a yes or no answer next time she saw you."

Charlie's just smiled and pulled a small box out of his pocket, "I remember Lieutenant."

There was only one plane on the deck for the Navy Seal to use, the rest were below deck to make room for all of the helicopters that were going to be used on the rescue operation. Everyone was looking toward the north as they watched for the Ospreys and Apache helicopters to arrive. The hospital ship the U.S.S. Mercy had just arrived and was taking the lead as it waited to get as close to shore as it could without being detected so the rescue could make trips faster.

Charles raised his hand and pointed out over the deck, "Here they come."

Admiral Mahoney gave out orders to his officers "Get those Ospreys and Apache refueled as quick as you can, so we can get those Doctors and Nurses over to the Mercy I have the feeling they will be needed over there if the shit hits the fan!"

Sandy O'Donnell and the rest of the Doctors and Nurses had just heard that once they have landed a Seal team would be taking off to parachute into the camp. Her heart got heavy when she had heard the news; she knew her man would be one of those parachuting into the camp. She thought she was ready for this after watching her mother all of those years when her dad was away on missions. But this was the man she wanted to spend the rest of her life and have children by it seemed different now.

Once the helicopter landed she got off to stretch her legs and the saw her brother John and Charlie walking toward her and Charlie was in full gear heavily armed.

Charlie walked within a couple feet of Sandy and got down onto one knee and held out his hand with the little box he had in his pocket. "Will you marry me?"

Sandy fought back some tears as she looked down at the Diamond ring in the little box, reaching out she took the box out of Charlie's hand and then looked down at him and wiped a tear off her cheek. "I will put this on my finger as soon as my dad and my little sister are safely on board, I feel as though they too should share this moment, I hope you understand?" She looked over at her brother and then back at Charlie, "I also want my dad to know the truth about what had happened to his family then my answer is yes, I will marry you."

Charlie stood up, "I personal will tell your dad the truth and I promise I will bring your dad and your little sister out of that hell hole, so I hope you have started planning out then wedding details?"

John looked at Charlie and then at Sandy, "If something happens, I will get them out!"

Sandy walked up to Charlie and gave him a big long hug and then a long deep kiss then stepped back and wiped another tear, "You be safe, and I'm looking forward to being your wife and raise your daughter, my love and maybe even having one or two myself."

Charlie's pulled Sandy back into his arms and gave her another long hug and kiss and then stepped back, then he turned and walked back to his team who were starting to board the plane.

John gave her sister a hug, I'll make sure Charlie comes back and dad and our little sister get out of that hell hole, you have my word on that!" Charlie then met up with is team as they started to suiting up for the jump.

A few minutes later Sandy got back onto the helicopter holding the little box with the ring close to the chest and she gave Charlie a little wave as they disappeared aboard.

Admiral Mahoney has walked down to talk to the doctors and nurses before they headed over to the U.S.S. Mercy, "I would like some nurses to volunteer to fly in during the rescue, just in case some need immediate medical attention!"

Doctor Ben Smith looked at his wife and she just nodded her head, she moved toward the Admiral with three other nurses.

A short time later Admiral Mahoney was standing in front of the Navy Seals and the Corpsman and he was holding a pair of night vision goggles. "I just heard from Ambassador Flannigan and he has two men in position with laser guns that will be fired just as you jump." Holding up the goggles, "With these you will be able to see the laser beams that will be crossing at the hole into the prisoners barracks." He took one more look over at everyone and then took a deep breath, "If you run into trouble, you will be on your own for a good couple hours before the Marines come, you will have no backup!" They all took one pair of the goggles as they boarded the waiting airplane.

On one hill watching the camp, is President Romani and Ambassador Flannigan and two of his Marines, one has a laser gun and the other is Sergeant Samarth Black and she is manning the radio. She turned and looked at both of them, " Sir, they are five minutes out."

Flannigan walked over and tapped the Marine with the laser gun on the shoulder and he fired up the laser so did the other Marine at their posts on the other hill.

Samarth used a pair of the night vision goggles to directing the Marine with the laser distance and height, until all of the lasers intersect right over the hole in the roof.

Once everything was lined up she cursed under her breath, she wished she could do more to help. She had a three-year old son back home in Kentucky herself. Looking up into the sky she was glad it was a moonless night, then she heard the airplane, just as the explosions started to go off from the oil drums.

CHAPTER 25

Sergeant John O'Donnell was sitting on the floor with his head in his hand trying to contemplate what was coming and not showing any fear. He just couldn't get the sound of Abbie's cries for help in the cave now it was going to on for a few hours. He was not sure how much more of this he could take the smell of death was getting to him; it had not beaten him yet but close. Now today, Macall lost her arm and Hadria and Sabeen in that damn sweatbox to die was almost too much.

Diane Mahoney gradually walked over to John and sat down next to him as she put her arm around his shoulders, "Sergeant we all know that you care about everyone here, but there was nothing we could do to help Abbie or the others. You know that the guards are looking for an excuse to hurt you to the point you can't recover, or kill you, Chavez's ordered them not to kill you don't matter to them. I know what some of the prisoners were signing today while the guards were putting the twins in the box!"

John just nodded his head yes slowly, "We have all seen so much death these last few years and I'm not sure I can take anymore."

Diane then looked around the barracks and saw her students waiting for her near the east wall walked over to them, stopping near Marie, who is a little over 8 months pregnant after she was gang raped by the guards, "Keep an eye on Sergeant, I think he maybe sick again."

Marie looked up at Diane sternly, "It's my job to keep an eye on him and I think it maybe his heart this time, teach!"

Diane nodded at Marie and then glanced back at John, then she went and sat with her students, she knew that John was the only thing holding them all together. She then looked at Janet, "I think you should go and try and cheer up your dad, or you could just sing to use."

Janet looked over at her dad and back at Diane and started to single softly.

John heard his daughter starting to sing softly as he looked around the room everyone went and sat by Janet. Marie slowly walking toward John and she does not look happy, these last eight mouths on a pregnant woman had been hard, "I for one want to fight tomorrow morning at roll call, just like everyone else, this has gone on long enough."

John gave her an unhappy look, "What about your baby?"

Marie looked down at her swollen belly, "My baby will not be a slave, like I have been here."

Before either one could say another word Juana walked over to them and handed John the piece of paper the driver had put in her pants, "The driver said that this was for you."

John took the paper out of Juana's hand and looked at it and read it and then looked at Marie, "It says help is on the way, but not when!"

Mahari Guerra interrupted them with a worried look on his face, "We have a problem, and I think Isabel is having an appendicitis attack?"

John slowly got up and walked over to Isabel who likes to lay under the opening in the roof so she can look at the stars and her nickname was stargazer.

John and Mahari both knelt down next to Isabel who was looking up at the stars and you could tell she was trying to hide her pain, suddenly she pointed up at the stars, "I see some dark angles coming for me, do not let them take me!" They moved her to a pad on the ground to assess her better.

A loud explosion erupted from the south of them and John looked up he thought he saw something too. Then more explosions went off, as if he had sudden recollection he realized what he was seeing was parachutes coming out of the sky down toward them one after another. He stood up in anticipation and finally knew help was coming, and this was just the beginning. As quickly and quietly as he could he spread his arms out motioning to people, "Move everyone away from this area!" Then it was as if that stupid hole in the roof was now a lifeline as the first parachute appeared.

John counted five parachutes landing in the barrack's the last, parachute got hung up on the roof and John and couple others rushed over and pulled the person down just as the explosions had stopped. John took both of his hands over his head pulling on his hair, and then turned to the prisoners to get to the front door. "What's going on out there?"

A few moments passed then one of the guards shouted back, "It's something you will have to clean up tomorrow morning, so go back to sleep." Followed by some drunken laughter.

John turned around to see the five parachutists most gear had already been unpacked and some were assessing some of the prisoners. "Thanks the heavens you are here, I had all but given up by now!"

Little Bear moved toward John and pointed at himself and then the other, Uncle, it's me Little Bear and this is Nighthawk, that's Sleeping Dog and this is Corpsman Amy Thomas and Master chief Charlie Brown. We are going to get all of you out safe, but you left us no choice we had to send a few of us in early." As relaying this he signed it at the same time.

John watched Corpsman Thomas looked around the barracks as if looking for someone. "I'm not leaving until everyone gets out of here."

Little Bear looked over at Nighthawk who was on the radio then back at John, "At dawn the Marines are coming in full force, I wonder if the guards want to surrender, then he grinned. We didn't want something stupid to happen before they got here. The food truck here yesterday had some cameras and a microphone on it so we knew what happen yesterday evening."

Many of the prisoners started to get riled up, but John quickly raised his hands to keep them quite Thomas opened her first aid kit and started working on Macall's arm. He went over to her side and put his arm on her shoulder, "How good are you?"

Without taking her eyes off of Macall's arm she started to clean it, "I'm the best, that is why I'm here!"

John looked toward sleeping Dog, "You finish this up I have someone you have to attend to and it cannot wait until morning! We think she is having an appendicitis attack? You have to help her!" Looking at Mahari who was kneeing next to Isabel, "Please don't let her die."

Corpsman Thomas just stared down at Isabel who looked like a helpless 6-year-old, she could tell she was in a lot of pain so she got down next to her and gave her a little something to ease it. She looked at Mahari and John; "I'm going to need some more light now!"

John knew the light would draw attention, then spotted Adriano and Chico both playing with the parachute that had gotten hung up, "Adriano, Chico, bring that parachute over here." Both Adriano and Chico slowly drug the parachute they were playing with over and with the help of Little Bear who knew what John had in mind started to set up. "Both of you stand on each side of Isabel with your hands up in the air, like tall trees." With the help of Little Bear, John pulled the parachute over both of Adriano and Chico and then turned toward Thomas, "Your operating room is ready, doctor." Thomas slowly entered the room that been made for her to operate on Isabel fashioned with as many lights as they had in their gear and pulled her supplies in with her.

Little Bear looked at John, "I need to talk to you about what is going to happen in the morning. I also need to talk to Raeanne Romani and anyone else you think we need to inform about the recue operation."

John called out, "Raeanne, Marie, Pablo." And waved them to come closer to them.

Chief Charlie Brown who had been checking out the barrack and then walked over to where they were. Once they are all together they all sat down on the floor to make plans.

Raeanne also bought Janet with her she was not sure why they needed her, but was happy to know that help was on the way. Janet moved closer to her dad and couldn't keep her eyes off of Little Bear she seemed cautious and a little scared.

Little Bear looked at Raeanne, "First President Chavez is dead and your daughter Angella Romani is now the new President of Enceladus, no one can know this until the rescue. She had asked for our help as she is afraid that once the guards find out that Chavez is dead they might start killing everyone.

John looked at Raeanne and Little Bear, "I need to tell you that today we were at the archaeology dig site near here and when we were leaving, there was a cave in and Abbie was trapped inside and they would not let me go back in to get her! We could hear her calling for help. You need to send someone to recue her before she dies in that damn cave."

Little Bear got up and went over to Nighthawk who was manning the radio and relayed the information, "I will see what can be done to help her."

Charlie took John and Janet aside, he was serious but you could see the gleeful anticipation in his face, "Sergeant I have information to give you about your family, there is no easy way to say this so I am just going to give it to you straight. They were not killed in a car accident, your wife retired from the Navy with the rank of Captain shorty after she found out that she was pregnant, by the way you have a daughter and your daughter dreams is to be the first female Navy Seal. She is a stubborn one, must take after you." He grinned at John. "Your son John is now a Marine Lieutenant and he is on the U.S.S. Nokomis he will be on one of the helicopters taking part in the rescue operation. Your daughter Sandy is a Navy Pediatric and right now she is aboard the U.S.S. Mercy you will be taken there for medical attention after we get out of here." He paused for a moment to let John process what he had told him, "Once you and Janet are both safely on board she promised to put on the engagement ring I had in my pocket, we have been dating for a couple years my little girl set us up on a blind date and it was love at first sight for me. One more thing, your son's wife is pregnant, you're going to be a grandpa."

Janet looked up at her dad dumbfounded, "I have two sisters?"

John just nodded his head yes as he smiled at her. Hey Charlie, you had better get us out of here or she might just have you court martialed."

John drawing on the floor a map of the camp with a stick that was lying around and pointed out to Charlie one of the buildings, "This building has all the records of everything that has happened here it is imperative that it not be destroyed and everything in it confiscated." Charlie nodded and then went over too Little Bear and Nighthawk and told him to relay the information over the Com.

CHAPTER 26

Sergeant Samarth Black was monitoring the radio traffic for the Navy Seals inside the barracks and the Nokomis, she turned and looked at both President Angella Romani and Ambassador Flannigan, "Where is the archaeologist caves? There is a young girl named Abbie trapped in it and she was reported to be alive!"

Rafael Lang looked at the map on the table and then looked up and pointed to the east of where they were, "It's about a mile from the camp due South West."

Samarth Black looked right at Flannigan, "Sir, I would like to go and help get her out, as a kid I was always crawling in old cave!"

Flannigan turned and looked at Angella who looked beaten down as she took a deep breath and leaned up against the table, "Rafael, do whatever you have to do to get her out of there before the Marines land in that damn camp in the morning!"

Flannigan just nodded his head yes looked at Sargent Black, "Get someone to man that radio." Sargent Black did and was already moving toward Rafael with a determine look on her face, and they took a couple men with her.

About ten feet down the pathway they passed two soldiers leading two older frightened men until they saw a United State Marines who look very scared but when they see a United State Marines passing them, their looks change to confusion and even more so when they saw Angella and Flannigan standing together looking down at something on a table and talking softly together.

Angella spotted the two older men and very slowly walked toward them and tried to make her voice as soothing as possible, "Gentlemen it's my job to inform you that President Chavez and all of his staff are deceased! I'm the acting President until we can hold new elections. I believe in free press and that is why you are here. I want you to document everything unless it is classified. I want it on the front page of your papers even if mistakes are made." She brought them over to get a better view, "Do you see over this small hill? "It's is a prison camp that holds over 400 men, women and children, and at sunrise the guards will be ordered to surrender or face the deathly consequences! What they don't know is that we are not alone." What she did not tell the reporters that a whole detachment of Marine helicopters would be on standby and platoons with boots on the ground ready to infiltrate if they do not surrender.

Rafael and Samarth and a few more got into an old truck and headed toward the archaeologist sight, they all hoped that the little girl was still alive.

Ben Black, could not get back to sleep after hearing all the explosions nearby so he had decided to check if his buyer for the dig had gotten a hold of him, he had lot of money to spend on rare items and never asked questions. Most of Ben's workers were also up and loading the last finds into a truck for them trip to the airport. Once he was out of this damn country he was not coming back and President Chavez would not see a penny from him again.

He spotted a truck pulling into his camp and wondered if Chavez found out about his leaving without him knowing. He was shocked to see a female U.S. Marine and other soldiers getting out of the truck, they looked like they had urgent business.

Samarth was surprised to see someone around but marched right up to Ben, "WHAT CAVE IS ABBIE IN?"

Ben looked around as if trying to think of something to say without being implicated and was thinking maybe he could talk his way out of this, "Abbie who?"

Samarth turned and gave a snide look at Rafael and the other soldiers were starting to approach, without another word she slammed her fist into Ben's stomach and made him double over, she was past the point of caring if she got into trouble. She took a step back and looked a the other workings, "I'm not going to asks again, what cave is she IN?" All the workers meekly pointed down the same pathway. Samarth started toward the pathway, but pointed at Ben, "Bring him with us, and maybe a couple others they can help us get her out!"

Rafael walked up to Ben and shoved him toward the pathway, "Get moving or I will shoot you where you stand myself!"

Holding his stomach, Ben said to Rafael, "I have lots of money, and some of it's your if you keep me away from that lunatic she's loco."

Rafael pulled his pistol out, "I said move it!" Ben directed the other workers standing there in shock, "Bring some shovels to the cave with you." They all started to follow down the pathway.

Samarth was running as fast as she could, it was dark and she felt her anger growing at every step as she approached the cave entrance that has some boards blocking it. She reached out with both hands and started to pull the boards away; She then entered the front of the cave, then she came to a wall of dirt that was chest high, she could just barely see the top of a head further back into the cave, and knew she was buried up to her neck, "Abbie!"

She pulled out a flashlight she shone it toward Abbie, just in time to see her eyes opening slowly; she got up on top of the dirt and started to crawl toward her as fast as she could.

Abbie heard someone shout her name and then saw a light move toward her as she heard a female shouting her name over and over. In a very weak voice she responded, *"I'm here, help me."*

As soon as Samarth reached Abbie she started to dig around her with her bare hands as fast as she could, she didn't want the dirt to fill back around her and swallow her up she had dropped the flashlight next to her. "I'm an United State Marine, your Sergeant sent me to get you out of here."

Abbie opened her eyes and looked up at her almost in shock, *"Marine like Sergeant?"*

"Yes, like your Sergeant." One of the others joined her with a shovel and he started digging. After digging a bit, Samarth reached into the hole and put her hands around Abbie under her armpits and pulled her out of the hole. With her arms around Abbie just totally wrapped herself around Samarth until out of the cave. It was not until then that Samarth realized Abbie was covered from head to toe in dirt and was completely nude. She took off her uniform jacket off, and wrapped it around Abbie. Abbie had a cut on her face and would need medical attention.

Abbie peered in the darkness and spotted Archaeologist Ben Black on his knees in front of a

Marine still holding his stomach. Slowly she walked over to Ben and held out her hand and in it was a small figurine she had dug out before the cave in.

Ben just stared at that figurine, wondering its value. He reached out to take it but Lang kicked his hand back, he then grabbed him up by the collar and pushed him back down the pathway, "Move."

Samarth get down on her knee and using her canteen to wipe Abbie face clean of the dirt. Then she swooped up Abbie in her arms and carried her down the pathway and set her gently into the back of the truck with Lang who had his pistol on Ben.

Abbie never took her eyes off Ben while in the back of the truck, until they come to a stop at base camp a couple of men opened the back gate with rifles pointed at Ben. "Get out and do not do anything stupid." One man then handcuffed and led Ben to the front of the truck. The other man held out his hand and gently said to Abbie, "Come on out, we will not hurt you." With the help of Samarth, Abbie rose and slowly walked to the back of the truck looking around. One down on the ground she was glued to Samarth.

Angella was talking to the reporters when she spotted Ben Black making his way to the tent, then she saw Abbie who was scared and holding Samarth's hand tight. She walked up to Ben and looked at Lang, "Take him to the prison and give him my old cell until his trial."

Ben just looked at Angella with pleading eyes, "I have contracts to do my work here and it's sanctioned."

Angella just waved him away, "Tell it to the judge I do not care about any contracts you had with Chavez."

Ben started to shout something but stopped when he felt Lang's pistol in his back, "Don't even think about it." He then lowered his head turned away toward the pathway, followed by Lang.

Once Ben is out of sight, the reporters started to move toward Abbie, but Samarth raised her hand to stop them as she moved in front of Abbie.

Angella seeing all of this moved up next to Samarth and then knelt next to Abbie, "You are safe here and I bet you're hungry?"

Abbie looked up at Samarth and then at Angella, "I eat after Grisel does as she is younger then me."

Angella gave Abbie a little smile, "What if your Sergeant says that it's ok to eat now." Abbie looked up at Samarth and then at Angella and then nodded her head yes.

Taking Abbie by the hand Samarth lead Abbie over to the radio and lets her talk to John for a few minutes and when she was done talking she led her to a small tent, where some food was stored. Opening a small cooler Samarth took out a sandwich and cut it in half and then handed Abbie one of the half. "Take some small bits." When Abbie opened her mouth to eat, Samarth saw that she had almost no teeth and that made her even madder at the people who ran that camp. Next she took a first aid kite and started to work on all of her cuts, as she got even madder as he looked like she may have been hit a few times.

John handed the microphone back to Little Bear and he was happy that Abbie was alive and safe and that made him feel a little better about everything but there was much more to worry at least one of his people was safe and that make he feel a bit better about.

Without warning everyone heard a quail sound coming from the front of the building from one of his lookouts; John stood up and looked at Little Bear, "Trouble!"

They all heard a whisper from the lookout, "Its Amor."

Amor hated being woke up from his sleep by those explosions had done just that, even after several beers. But he knew that maybe a girl's charms would work. He took a drag off his joint as he neared the door to the barrack he took out the key. Unlocking the door, he stepped in and stopped dead in his tracks when he saw that damn Sergeant and four other men all dressed in black and armed. Raised his arms as he looked at John and the weapons, "Who are these guys and how did they get in here?"

John took two steps out in front of the Navy Seals, "If you surrender you will live to see the sun raise."

Amor blinked a few times to make sure he was really seeing this and not dreaming. He reached for his pistol in his shoulder hoister. But he could not get it drawn before something was sticking out of his neck. It was the last thing he saw as he dropped to the floor dead.

Little Bear walked over to Amor and bent over and pulled his knife out of Amor's neck and then pulled out Amos's pistol and tossed it to John, "Catch, you might need this."

John slowly walked up to Amor and just shook his head then he turned and looked at two of his fellow prisoners, "Drag this piece of shit over to the shit pile."

CHAPTER 27

Meanwhile back at the White House the congressional majority leaders were gathering for a briefing they were not happy to have they're Four of July holiday ruined. Senator Barbara Thomas looked at Senator Sam Hill, "I heard that Vice-President Cook had to cancel a fund raiser because of the flu, or something.

Sam looked around the hallway as they all waited for someone to take them to see the President, "At his age it could just about anything."

Abruptly the Brigade General Artie Goodman walked toward them holding a box, and he looked troubled. Goodman stood right in front of the leadership, "Before I take you to the war room, I need you to turn off your cell phones and pagers, and put them in this special box that will jam signals."

The majority leaders started talking all at once, "Why the war room and not the oval office, why do we have to turn our cell phone and pagers off?"

Goodman raised his hand to and addressed them, "If you do not like it? You can wait here, until the President holds a press conference later in the morning!"

Senator Thomas raised both of her hands as she turned around and faced the leadership, "I'm turning mine off, obviously, this is important and I need to see what is going on, if you want to wait here you can. But I'm going to the war room, NOW!" She then turned around and pulled out her cell phone turning it off and placed it in the box Goodman was holding.

The rest started to follow suit and do the same thing then Brigade General Goodman turned, "Follow me."

As they neared the elevator they saw Marines on both sides of the door on guard. The doors opened, a Navy Captain exit and so does a young girl in a Girl Scout uniform.

If you lived in Washington D.C. for any length of time you could not miss seeing the Navy Captain's face smiling on billboards or TV ads for her construction business, but she was not smiling right now.

Margie walked up the Majority leader's, her eyes burning with fire right into your soul, "If you stop this operation I will go to every VFW and American legend and tell them that you caused the deaths of many men, women and children. One of them being my husband a United State Marine!" She stepped closer until right in front of Thomas and held two fingers about a inch apart, "You are this close to losing my respect your daughter is the bravest Navy corpsman I know right now, and that is your only saving grace. Part of this is your fault your background checks are substandard and your aid Jim Brown is in the drug business a murderer and a rapist wait until you watch the video's I just saw!" Then she turned and marched off but stopped and looked back over her shoulder, "Just remember what I said earlier and what I will do if you try and stop this!" She took Susan by the hand they both exited the White House.   While she stood outside waiting for a car Margie pulled out her cellphone and made a call, "Dad, I want you to go to the holiday Inn and pickup Janet and Albert O'Donnell and bring them to my house, I'll explain when I get there. Paul Blue has the key to the house, once you are there turn on the TV on to any new channel." Not waiting for a response she hung up as a car was pulled up.

CHAPTER 28

On the Nokomis Admiral Mahoney has gathered all personal taking part in the recue operation in one of the bays. He has a big picture of the camp on a big screen. Major Ann Morgan walked on to the platform on one of the stairs everyone stood at attention until she told the Marines at ease, "This will be your finial briefing on the upcoming mission. Of course we will give them the option to surrender (this got a few chuckles from the personal) if not, we will hit them in three waves. She used a laser pointer as she spoke. The first wave will be made up of five apache helicopters and their job will be to hit all of the towers and the front gate, and the guard's main building. The second wave will be made up of four Super Stallion helicopters and their job will be to get the Marines inside of the prisoners building and secure the surrounding area. The third wave will be make up of the Ospreys, Lieutenant Becker we need you to come in over the wire as low as you can with four Marines and get the two girls out of the sweatbox." Then pointed to another building, "Once Lieutenant Becker is on the ground, Sergeant Jim Davis and Lance Corporal Bonne Cook will go and secure the records building there is evidence, I can's stress enough how important this is."

Lieutenant Amy Becker stood up and looked around at all her colleges then up at Major Morgan, "May I openly speak sir?" Major Morgan gave the go ahead with a nod. "If they do not surrender, I do not care how much gunfire I take, I'm not leaving until I have a loaded helicopter with prisoners and if something should happen and I cannot take off, I will join the Marines on the ground, my helicopter is armored as the prisoners should be safe. If any of my crew does not like this idea, do not get on this chopper!" She pointed to the American flag on her shoulder, "These colors do not run and neither will I." All of the men erupted with a roar of excitement and from the Marines she got "Semper Fi." Major Morgan raised both of her hands and signaled everyone to be quite with a large smile. "Thank you Lieutenant Becker, now let me get on with the briefing." She turned back toward the screen and continued. "Along this road are mines and also the camp itself." She took a deep breath and looked at all of the Marines again. "When acting President Romani addresses the people of Enceladus and tells them that President Chavez is dead, she will give the option for the guards to surrender to the trucks that will be on route from her side. The first two trucks will be controlled remotely just in case they do not. If the guards fire on these trucks, you are to initiate the first wave without warning and in the words of acting President Romani, send them all to STRIGHT TO HELL! You are to get as many of the prisoners out as fast as you can and make sure they receive medical attention. You need to keep them from panic we don't want anyone killed in the crossfire. The good guys should be wearing orange vests and they know the consequences of any sudden moves. Once the camp is secure the third wave will come in and get the rest of the prisoner out. There was a brief pause, "Any questions?" Not hearing any but seeing a lot of concentration on the men decided enough said, "Good, now get something to eat as we lift off in zero three hundred hours, DISMISSED." Zero two thirty hours later Lieutenant John O'Donnell walked over to the helicopters to check on the crew and to hand out orders. He then stopped in front of Lieutenant Becker and gave her a salute, "Permission to join you?"

Lieutenant Becker returned his salute, "Any time Lieutenant." John climbed onto the helicopter and shook the hands of some of her crewmembers that were ready and heavily armed.

Admiral Mahoney looked down from the bridge as all of the rescue helicopters were waiting for the signal to take off, then over the intercom the priest on board a prayed. General Mike Heckman got onto one of the of the Super Stallions and he was also heavily armed. Then the Admiral looked down at his watch and nodded his head at Ensign Tammie Parker, she raised the flare gun and fired it into the night sky.

On the U.S.S. Mercy Captain Gregory Mahoney was in front of his chief of staffs with Doctor Dale Thompson at his side, "Everyone listen up and we have get his right, Chief Joni Wells, I want the cooks ready to feed the prisoners you are in charge of the mess hall, and remember they won't be in good shape and have not eaten in a while, nurses will be assigned to assist with feeding and bathroom attendance."

Thompson then took a step forward, "When they start to arrive I want the ones that are not hurt taken straight to the showers, given clean clothes and then fed. Triage will happen on the deck first, the first, sending the worst ones right into surgery."

Gregory looked over his people, "All hands-on deck, when we have incoming wounded. Any personal caught not doing their job, I will personal put fifty pounds of weights on their legs and then throw them over board!"

Doctor Sandy O'Donnell slowly stood up, "May I speak sir?"
Mahoney nodded, "I have shown most of you a photo of my Dad and Sister and I would like to be informed about their arrival."

Gregory waited until Sandy was seating again, "I want everyone to be ready for the worst, but hope for the best, remember most of them are very young and there are lot of children, they will be frightened, so be gentle." He looked around the room, "Alright then, everyone to their posts, it is going to be a long day so make sure everyone is well rested, take shifts."

Sandy waited for everyone to leave the area before she did and then walked outside just in time to see the helicopter-flying overhead toward shore. She walked to the middle of the landing pad and raised her hands out stretched to the sky with palms up, tilted her head back, "Sprits of my ancestors, both Apache, and Irish hear your daughter's prayer, today good men and women are going into battle to help those who cannot help themselves, I ask of you to bring everyone home safely." Then she lowered her head and hands and was startled when she heard a voice speak out. "I think they heard you." She turned around she saw Father Tony Gamble looking up at sky and pointing with his pipe. Sandy looked back up just in time to see a meteor shower and it almost looked like it formed a cross as they fell toward shore.

Father Gamble walked toward her as he lit his pipe, "You must have a lot of friends in high places."

She put her hand on his shoulder and they walked back inside, "Dad always talked to his ancestors and mom had the family in church every Sunday. It was not easy being Apache and Irish and Italian. But it made interesting and entertaining family gatherings." Father Gamble giggled.

CHAPTER 29

Margie and Susan exit the car at a mall parking lot. Four other cars were waiting for them, two FBI, one DEA and NCIS. One of the DEA agents was Little Bear's wife Cindy Humming-bird Smith she approached Margie, "I had to be here, I wanted to make sure that they pay for what they have done to your family and others by bring drugs into this country."

Margie gave Cindy a big hug and then whispered, *"Your husband and his men parachuted into the camp last evening."*

Cindy nodded her head and looked up into the night sky, "I know the ancient ones told me." She then led Margie and Susan over to where all of the other agents were waiting.

FBI agent Harrison Hill pulled out some papers, "Both Browns have permits to carry so be careful and here are some of the charges they will be charge with, drug running, rape, murder and money laundering." He looked at Margie, "They will be getting to restaurant Homeport just as the Marines go in, they have reservations for three so we believe the will be meeting with someone. We want to take them down before they can communicate with the camp and warn them.

Margie walked up to Hill, "Sir may take lead? I want to be the one to tell them that they are under arrest. You have my word that I will not lay a hand on them."

Hill looked around at the other agents and nodding his head, "Roger that, but remember if they try something get out of the way fast I got your six. Everyone weapons check we have one hour before the Marines hit that camp!"

Margie pulled Susan close and started planning what she is going to say to those two bastards, she almost hoped they would try something, because all she wanted to do was get her hands on just one of them.

CHAPTER 30

Sergeant O'Donnell was quietly moving around the barracks making sure everyone was spread out, just in case the guards started shooting at random into the barracks. He then stopped and looking down at Isabel who had Corpsman Thomas's vest spread out across her abdomen and she looked very pale, he put his hand on her shoulder, "We are going to try and get you out on one of the first helicopters that comes in."

Isabel looked up at John and with a weak voice, "Will you help me to find new parents, in America and maybe some of my friends too?"

He looked down at her, "I will see what I can do, but no promise Okay?"

Isabel nodded her head and smiled at Daniela who was next to her and she does not look good as well, she had been trying fast lately.

CHAPTER 31

Senator Thomas was seated at a desk trying to clean the front of her sticky shirt. All she can think about was what some bad choices she made for her top aide and that her daughter was in that building surround by those evil men. This may put an end to her career in the senate once everyone fines out about Jim Brown and his brother Jack. She should have looked more closely into Jim's spending after he started showing up with all of those expense cars and cash. She watched as the President was having her press secretary work on a speech, she would be holding a press briefing within the next two hours.

President Jones walked over and sat down on the edge of the desk, "I wish I did not have to show you and the leadership those video's but everyone needs to see what kind of men we are dealing with." Putting her hand on Thomas's shoulder, "You are still my best friend and nothing will every changes that. The FBI would like to search his desk, to see if there is any information in it about the camp or his drug business." Thomas just nodded her head she hoped there was nothing in his desk, but senate business. She wondered if the voters would understand that she did not know where he got his money. But she was going to have the IRS check everyone of her accounts once this was done to make sure everything was legal.

CHAPTER 32

Lieutenant John O'Donnell had weapons check for all on board, four of his men were on the ropes ready to make the jump and get the girls out of the sweatbox. He looked out the side of the helicopter soon it will be sunrise and then acting President will be giving her speech telling them to surrender and if they do not, they will go in.

Acting President Romani was going over her speech and she watched some of her men setting up a Microphone, next to the Marine sniper, his rifle looking down into the camp. Sergeant Black was kneeling next to Abbie who was trying to look over the small hill at the camp below. Both reporters were busy jotting things down on paper as fast as they could and listing to everyone who quietly spoke about the coming raid.

Master Sergeant Joe Pederson was setting up a new radio with a wider range and was hooked up to the local radio stations.
Ambassador Flannigan was on another radio talking to the helicopters as they neared the camp.

Romani saw that Flannigan was pointing toward Pederson he held up the microphone for her. She moved toward the radio with a heavy heart because she knew that they would not surrender, but she had to try. She took the microphone and looked over the small hill, taking a deep breath, she then pressed the button "People of Enceladus, my name is Angella Romani and I'm your new President. President Chavez is dead and I would like all the men at Camp Hell to surrender to the trucks that are now making their way to your camp. If you do not surrender you will face the deadly consequences for your action, surrender and you will be treated fairly."

The Marine sniper reported, "They are all running into one large group near their main building and it looks like they are shouting something at the men in the towers!" Suddenly the lead truck was blown up and then she saw tracer fire going toward the prisoners building from the towers and their main building. The Marines opened fire into the camp, towers were hit by rocket fire from the Apache helicopters and helicopters started to land.

Grabbing the microphone with both of her hands and shouting into it, "Those are United State Marines you pissed off, DAMN YOU ALL TO HELL!"

Lieutenant Amy Becker flipped up her night vision goggles; it was no longer night with the entire area lit up by explosions going on. She pushed her chopper to fly low and as fast as she crossed over the wire. Once over the wire she dropped even lower so the Marines could get to the two girls in the sweatbox. She then banked to the right and landed as close as she dared to the prisoners building. Looking straight ahead she could now see that the guards building was nothing but a pile of burning rubble some men wearing orange jackets starting to move around it firing as they go.

Sergeant Paul Thorston and the three Lance Corporals who jumped with him took off toward the sweatbox. Just before Thorston had jump off the ropes he thought he saw someone shooting at the sweatbox. But now he was running toward the sweatbox and no longer sews anyone shooting. Once he was at the sweatbox he reached for the latch to open it and spotted a hole near the latch with blood coming out of it.

Thorston opened the top of the sweatbox and shouted over all of the shooting, "UNITED STATE MARINES, WE ARE HERE TO GET YOU OUT OF HERE."

Thorston barely heard a small weak voice over all of the commotion, *"My sister is hurt."* He reached in and as careful as he could pull out he first girl and then the other one. One of the girls had been hit in her hip and he looked at Lance Corporal Blair Keith, "You take one and I will take the other one." Looking at the other two Lance Corporals, "COVER FIRE!"

Becker looked over and saw that the men had the two girls out of the sweatbox and were running toward her helicopter as fast as they could.

Sergeant Jim Davis and Lance Corporal Bonnie Cook were off and running toward the building before the helicopter had even landed. When they neared, the record building they both saw a man exit rapidly trying to raise his rifle at the same time. Both Jim and Bonnie dropped to one knee and opened fired and then headed back toward the building. Bonnie was the first one inside followed by Jim and she stopped in her tracks when she saw what was on one of the monitors. Grabbing her knife as she turned to head back out, but was stopped by Jim. "He is dead so you cannot hurt him any more!"

"I do not care, I'm going to cut his balls off for that!" Bonnie pointed at the monitor with her knife.

Jim looking at the monitor, "I can take care of this building, you go and get that girl out of there if you can find her" Bonnie headed to the prisoners building. When Bonnie was gone he slammed his elbow into the monitor.

Jim knelt in the doorway with his weapon drawn as he watched Bonnie head toward the prisoner building, hoping she finds the girl still alive and well.

Lieutenant O'Donnell jump off the helicopter right behind Lance Corporal Doug Pike, who was 250 pounds of pure muscle, he headed straight toward one of the walls in the building and went right through it and Lieutenant O'Donnell was right behind him and the first think that hit him was that awful smell that almost took his breath away. He moved off to the side to let the other Marines enter the building and made the entryway even bigger. Doing a quick look around he spotted a young boy, who has been shot in the leg; he picked him up and headed out of the building to get him to safety.

Sergeant O'Donnell slowly stood up when the big explosions stopped and all he heard was small arms fire and saw Marines coming through the walls and the front door. Looking down he saw that Janet was holding onto his leg and she was looking scared. Off to his left he saw Corpsman

Thomas standing up shouting at two Marines with stretchers to come and get Isabel.

Thomas bent over and reached under Isabel shoulders as one Marine picked her up by the legs and then set her on the stretcher as genital as they could and then two Marines carried her out and onto one of the waiting helicopters. She then moved over to some of the others who were wounded and giving them aid before they were carried out. Looking over her shoulder at the Sergeant O'Donnell who has now dropped down onto one knee holding his side, he was in a lot of pain.

At the same time, Lieutenant O'Donnell also saw his dad go down on to his knee and Janet is trying to hold him up screaming for help. He got to his dad just as two of the Navy Seal, Nighthawk and Little Bear get to him at the same time.

Sergeant O'Donnell, was fighting to stay upright he saw a Marine Lieutenant standing in front of him and on the Marine's shirt he saw the name, O'Donnell on his uniform and he knew it was his son, grabbing the front of his sons uniform he yelled, "Get your sister out of here NOW!" His son picked up Janet and headed out with her as she screamed that she wanted to stay and help her daddy.

Just a few feet away from them Sergeant Robert Kane did not see anymore wounded or hurt people. He approached a small group of kids and reached out to carry one of the girls out but as he was reaching for her she raised a small stick and in broken English said, "I will walk out of here!" From behind him he heard Sergeant O'Donnell in a weak voice, "Let her walk out, I promised her she would someday walk out of here."

Kane took one step back as the little girl stood up and the first thing he saw was that she had a bent leg and needed the stick to walk upright. The little stick was being held together with just some cloth and twine. Stay two feet behind just in case she falls, but she make it out and then at the rear of the helicopter she shouted at the burning building, "I told you I would walk out of here someday!" He picked her up and put her into the helicopter, she was so brave just like his wife was after being putting into her wheelchair for the first time after her diving accident. He turned and headed back into the building to get more people out even though he would never get her out of his mind.

Nighthawk and Little Bear are trying pickup up Sergeant O'Donnell, but he is fighting them, "I will be the last one out of here so let me go!"

Off to his left he hears Marie Otto, "You are leaving right how Sergeant!" He turned to say something to her, but the first and last thing he saw was a fist heading toward his head.

Sergeant O'Donnell fell back into Nighthawk's arms out cold and Marie looked at Nighthawk, "Get him out of here, before he wakes up." Nighthawk just stared at a very pregnant woman as he watched her shaking her fist. Both Nighthawk and

Little Bear grab Sergeant O'Donnell and head for the nearest exited and a waiting helicopter.

Hallmar climbed out one of the back windows to escape the Marines. Taking a deep breath, he headed under the wire and toward the pathway though the minefield at a fast run without looking up.

Major Ann Morgan was flying her apache near the guard's building, when she spotted someone climbing out of a window. Knowing that there is a minefield she figured that his guard must know a path through it. She let him get about fifteen feet into the minefield before she opened up and watches as the ground all around the man exploded, sending him flying and setting off more mines. "You can run but you cannot hide from the Marines." She then turned and put a ten second burst into the window he had climbed out of, knocking the rest of the building down.

Nurse Jill Smith was trying to move around the Super Stallion helicopter checking all the former prisoners who had been shot or were hurt and doing triage, they were heading to the Mercy. She had never seen so many people wounded or shot. Leaning over the girl who had the vest covering her she pulled it off, and saw it was the girl, who had her appendix taken out and it looked like she was being held together with glue and safety pins. She radioed the Mercy to be ready for her the girl and relayed the injuries for the medics on standby she prayed that everyone would be okay once they landed. She looked around and saw a lot of scared faces but no one was crying it was almost eerily quiet; some were just staring at her and the other corpsman on board.

President Romani was just shaking her head as she watched the Marine landing and engaging the guards that survived the opening attack. She cannot believe how fast the Marines got onto the ground and the guard's main building reduced to rubble. She saw that Abbie was holding onto Sergeant Black as tight as she could look over the hill at the camp below and the destruction both reporters were busy writing and watching the Marine sniper who was busy finding targets and firing. One of the helicopters that had just taken off was heading their way and landed on the other side of them.

Sergeant Black lifted Abbie and carried her toward the helicopter the side door opened and they waved for her to carry Abbie over to them. Abbie stared at the helicopter with wide eyes, as she held onto Sergeant Black even tighter. Then she saw Sergeant O'Donnell inside she handed Abbie to one of the crewmembers, "You will be safe with them now." She watched as the helicopter took off and for some reason she felt a hole in her heart.

Captain Mahoney was listing to the radio on the bridge as he waited for the helicopter arrival with the former prisoners and he was not happy to what was being relayed. Picking up the microphone, "All hands-on deck prepare for incoming wounded with litters." Picking up his binoculars he scanned the early morning sky looking for the coppers. Then he spotted the first one in the distance and they all started coming one after the other, and he knew they were moving fast. He looked down onto the deck he saw a lot of his crewmembers waiting for the choppers and are ready to move everyone inside to be assessed as fast as possible. On all four side of the deck there were triage to set up to treat those who were in critical condition.

Even before the first Stallion's wheels touched the desk his crew was getting everyone out and onto gurneys and inside in haste. By the time the third one landed his medical bay was almost full and then he saw his niece Diane being helped off one of the helicopters and she looked like hell, he wanted to go down there, but he did not want to get in the way of the work being done.

Patty Brown was watching the choppers landing and Captain Ben Mahoney was right there she could not believe what she was seeing, even after 10 years as an ER nurse in Chicago busiest hospital, she was shocked.

Dr. Susan O'Donnell was looking down at Isabel, she was going to have to open her back up and start cleaning her up and fix some of the bleeders inside, and make sure she does not get an infection, she saw that the corpsman did a great job taking her appendix out. She leaned over Isabel, "I'm going to fix you up good as new, and I need for you to sleep for a little while first." She glance up for a moment and saw a lot of people who have been shot, she prayed that her sister and dad were safe and finished up on Isabel and then moved on to the next one. After a bit a nurse put her hand on her shoulder, "Your sister is on board and is safe. Your dad is on his way in and he is not good, they are not sure but maybe a heart attack!" Her heart sunk and she fought to keep standing, then started to work on the next patient a young man's wounded leg, which was hit in two places.

Sergeant O'Donnell was holding Abbie's hand as they landed he saw the door open and he made it. For the first time in a long time he felt safe, but he was still hurting. Dr. Dale Thompson having heard that Sergeant O'Donnell was hurt was at the door when it opened, he could tell that he was indeed in a lot of pain as he was clutching his chest with one hand. One female crewmember helped Abbie out of the helicopter and seeing that she was not hurt carried her straight inside the Mercy, and made sure she was okay. Two other crewmembers slowly slid Sergeant O'Donnell out and onto a gurney as Dr. Thompson grabbed his hand and then with one look, "Get him inside STAT!" Keying his Microphone so Dr. O'Donnell will not hear him, "Dr. Edwin you have a heart attack victim, its Sergeant O'Donnell."

CHAPTER 33

Margie and the agents pulled up to the Homeport about time the raid started and Margie was the first one out of her car, follow by Susan. Margie walked right into the establishment to the receptionists who happen to be Dawn Johnson. She put her hands on the desk, "Where are Jim and Jack Brown?"

Dawn just took a step back as Margie was in her Captain's uniform. Susan was in her girl Scott uniform and they both looked like they were about to explode, she turned to her right and pointing, "They are both on the outside patio with a guest."

Margie just turned and stormed toward the patio with ten agents close behind her and she didn't stop until she was at the doorway to the patio. Stopping in the doorway she saw both Brown's and another man she saw there sitting at the back of the patio and the unidentified man was handing Jim a big brown envelope and they handed him a thick white envelope. Now she was seeing red, she recognized what the brown envelope was and what it meant to her and her company. She held up her hand to keep the other agents back at the doorway and she and Susan headed straight toward the Brown's and their guest.

Jack Brown looked up and saw Margie and Susan heading toward them and he swore under his breath as he looked at his brother, "Trouble."

Jim saw Margie heading toward them and he tried to return the envelope to the man who was looking panicked and a bit pale.

Margie stopped behind the mysterious man and looked down at him, "That better not be my bids for the new hangers at JFK?"

Jack gave her a little laugh and noted that Margie was in her Navy uniform and Susan was in her Girl Scout uniform so he tried to change the subject, "The Navy must be scarping the bottom of the barrel to call you up."

The unidentified man looking toward the nearest exit, "I need to use the bathroom."

Margie just put her right hand on his shoulder holding him in place, "Just stay here until I'm done having a nice chat with your friends here."

Margie stared straight at the brothers and in a very firm voice, "You two are going to jail for a very long time and its not for stealing my bid for the new hangers a JFK! It's for murder, rape and drug running, just for starters! I'm sure that NCIS and the FBI will come up with more charges." She reached into her pocket and took out a picture and handed it to Jack, "Will you tell me who these people are in this picture?"

Jim leaned over and swore at her, he saw who was in the picture and Jack snickered, "It looks like a father and daughter at a nudist camp and I do not know them."

Margie moved to the side of Jack and Jim and grabbed hold of the table and flipped it over, she gave that look that could kill look, and in a shaking voice as all three men stood up, "That man is my husband, best friend and the father of my children who I love with all of my heart! You put him in that hellhole and right now, real god-fearing Marines have landed at this camp! If you are wondering, I will tell you. Your friend President Chavez was arrested and shot and acting President Angella Romani asked for the United States to send in the Marines to help free the prisoner at Camp Hell!" Pointing at the picture, "That girl's mother was the little sister of President Romani and you murdered her!" Clenching her fists at her sides, "Her name is Janet Lightfoot O'Donnell and she is my husband's daughter!" Then she stood back and waited as they were slowly surrounded. Then she took a deep breath, "I should also tell you that your friend President Chavez videotaped everything you did at the camp and I mean everything!"

Jack started to reach into his coat pocket; "I had better call our lawyer then."

But before he could get his hand into his coat he found himself looking down the barrel of a weapon. "Let me get your phone sir you do not want to make any mistakes!" Cindy Humming Bird slowly reached out and pulled his coat back and everyone saw his phone along with a small pistol in a shoulder harness.

Jim cursed under his breath at him, "Stupid."

FBI agent Harrison Hill pulled Jim's coat back and he saw that he too had a pistol in a shoulder harness, "I'll take that so you do not do anything stupid either." He disarmed him and Agent Bird disarmed Jack.

Agent Bird handed the pistol to another agent, put her own away and handcuffed his hands behind his back, "My husband is a Navy Seal, he parachuted into that camp last night and he is also related to Sergeant O'Donnell."

Once they were both handcuffed Margie moved until she was standing in front of them and just staring at them with dark eyes, "You will never get out of jail! If you do just remember I pour a lot of concrete and my building do not fall down easy!" She then looked at the other man who was still holding the envelope and was shaking like a leaf. She grabbed it out of his hand and looked at it, then handed it to FBI agent Hill. "Give this to his boss and let him handle this."

He looked over his shoulder as Hill was putting handcuffs on him too, "Let make a deal?"

Agent Hill just pushed him toward the doorway, "Asks someone who gives a damn, I'm a retired Marine." There was puddle of water where he had been standing.

As both Jack and Jim are being escorted out Jimmy Johnson was standing in the doorway with his arms crossed and a meat cleaver in his hand, He then buried the clever deep into the wall near the doorway, just before they exited the building.

Margie slowly sat down and looked at one of the waitresses, "Could I get a glass of ice tea please?"

Susan sat down next to her mother and holding up her hand, "Could I get one too please?"

After a few minutes Margie looked at Jimmy and Dawn who were busy keeping the other guests away from them, they both finished their ice tea and then looked at Dawn "Could you find someone to drive us home? I want to be home when my husband calls me." Margie then stood up and pulled out her phone and called her brother, "Billy I need you to get as many of your police cadets and go to my place, my place is going to be crawling with reporters and I want you to keep them off of my yard. Big John is coming home and he is alive!" Not waiting for her brother to ask her anything she hung up and headed toward the exit holding Susan hand with a look of pride on her face.

Dawn just looked at Jimmy with a large smile, "I'll get the car."

Jimmy followed them out and turned toward one of the valet parking people, "An investigator will be showing up to tow those cars out of here, they may have evidence in them.

CHAPTER 34

President Romani was standing on the hill looking down at the camp as the last helicopter left, then she turned and looked at Rafael, "I want to go down there, right now!"

Rafael looked also down the hill and then conveyed orders, "Get car, we are heading down there."

Romani slowly walked down the small ridge and looked at Ambassador Flannigan, "Would you like to join me?"

Flannigan nodded his head and saw that the Marines were packing up equipment, "Head back to the compound and I will join you later."

Sergeant Samarth Black, walked up to Flannigan and stood at attention, "Sir I would like to join you?" He gave permission by a nod and they all started to walk down to the waiting cars, Sergeant Black kelp remembering Abbie's rescue and how helpless she looked when she pulled her out of that damn cave and it reminded her of her own son back home about the same age, and how they were so fragile.

General Mike Rohrer was talking to one of the Enceladus new General's while Lieutenant O'Donnell watched some of the Enceladus soldiers carry the dead over to an area near the main entrance. One soldier had a book with each guard's information and photo and was checking off each one. Two soldiers pulled what is left of the gate open so more trucks could enter the camp.

Lieutenant O'Donnell looked up the road and stood near the panel that opened the fire pit, two cars came into the camp guarded by two people on each side. He took off his helmet and attached his bayonet on his rifle and then slamming it into the ground with his helmet on the butt of it.

Sergeant Samarth Black was standing guard on the second car that held Ambassador Flannigan, she just stared at the camp as it looked a lot different now, the main building was a pile of burning rubble, and there was a lot of chaos and destruction. She watched as all the Marines were lining up with the Enceladus and some of them were so young they looked like kids with rifles.

President Romani stepped out of the car and looked around at the mayhem, she felt some tears rolling down her face and thought of her sister giving birth here and dying here. Her mother was here also and she felt it was her fault, but she was free now, so was her niece. She spotted a Marine standing over by the panel next to his over-turned rifle and helmet and she slowly walked over to him, then she saw his name on his uniform, "Are you related to Sergeant O'Donnell?"

He stood at attention, "He's my father, President."

Romani lowered her head a bit, "I'm so sorry about everything that happen to your dad while he was here."

Lieutenant O'Donnell just raised his arm and pointed at the burning rubble, "It's not your fault, those that I blame are dead or in jail. I'm sure my dad feels the same way, as does the rest of my family, we are just thankful that you let us get him out so he can come home." Then he looked down at his rifle, "I personally carried my little sister, your niece out of there and put her on one of the Super Stallions." He then Saluted the President and stuck out his hand, "I would like to shake your hand

Madam President for everything you did today to save my dad, my sister and everyone else that was suffering here."

Romani shook his hand and turned to look at all of the other Marines who were lining up and her own troops were lining up with them. She turned and walked over to General Rohrer and shook his hand, "Thank you General for saving everyone who were being held here."

Rohrer nodding his head toward the Enceladus general, "I was just telling General Lustig here that none of the rescues were dead. We carried out a hell of a lot of wounded people, but no one was killed here other than the guards Madam President."

Romani looked at all the men lining up, "I would like to shake everyone's hand, before they head back to the Nokomis."

Rohrer turned and leads Romani toward the Marines who were all standing at attention. "At ease Marines." And one by one she thanked each one of them.

The third Marine she shook hands with was Sergeant Robert Kane who looked at General Rohrer, "Permission to speak Sir?"

General Rohrer answered, "Go ahead Sergeant."

Kane took a deep breath, "Madam, what is going to happen to the kids? There was one girl I would love to adopt Madam. I have a trust fund waiting for me and it yours if I can adopt her."

Romani was at a loss for words and saw other Marines nodding their heads too; "I will bring it forward to the cabinet and take it to a vote. But I will let you know as soon as I can, Sergeant."

Kane just nodded his head, "I understand Madam."

Once Romani shook all the Marines hands that had lined up she, Ambassador Flannigan and both General's walk into the barrack that is now empty. They all took a few steps inside and looked around as soon as the smell hit her she covered her nose and mouth and left the building as fast as she could. "Take lots of picture of this place and then burn it down!" She wiped a few tears from her face, "General Rohrer, "I know that the doctors on the Mercy are very busy right now so sometime tomorrow I would like to speak with your Sergeant O'Donnell myself.

CHAPTER 35

Paul Blue watched from his front window as a van pulled up into Margie's driveway, both of her parents get out and then when the van door opened, he saw Janet lightfoot O'Donnell rolling out in her wheelchair followed by her husband Albert O'Donnell. He opened his front door as Margie's dad, Frank Bender who looked worried and his wife Sue helped Albert and Janet up to the house. He was not sure if he should tell them what he had just heard from Jimmy about Big John or wait until Margie got home.

Frank watched as Paul headed toward him, "Margie told me that you have the keys to her house?"

Paul pulled the keys out of his pocket and flipped them to Frank, "I just heard that Margie and Susan will be home shortly."

Frank looked over his shoulder and then back at Paul, "Do you know what is going on?"

Paul looked and smiled at Janet and Albert who were waiting, "I'll let Margie tell you all about it, but its good news, Sir."

Frank looked down at the keys and then back up at Paul, "I will have to take you word for that when she called me she sounded very worried about something."

Just then Margie's little brother Billy pulled up with a second large van, about fifteen police cadets jumped out and stood in front of Billy who was handing them police tape. Paul's daughter Amy came up behind him, "Dad I just heard that the President would be specking in about a half hour." Turning to walk back into his house he looked over his shoulder at Frank who was opening the door to Margie house and just smiled, it would be good to see Big John home again.

Shortly after that Paul spotted Dawn's car coming down the street and pull in behind the van Susan got out and ran toward the house. Margie got out of the car and at a fast pace walked up to the front porch and hugged Albert and then sat down in front of Janet.

Tears ran down her face as she looked up at Janet, "Big John is coming home and he is alive." She wiped her tears away and took a deep breath, "I have to tell you about how they tortured him, but before I tell it was worst then any Apache or British King could think of. He was order by his captors to have sex with a young lady named Mary, but he refused and was then beaten severely, until Mary could not take it anymore. Nine months later Mary gave birth to a little girl, John named Janet lightfoot O'Donnell." She looked up at Albert who is fighting back tears as he listened intently to Margie holding onto the handles of his wife's wheelchair. She then reached up and took Janet's hands into her own, "I now have to tell you the worst part. At the camp, the men who betrayed John came to the camp, he was being held at." Her mother had her hand over her mouth, "They ordered onto her knees and tied her hands behind her behind and wanted her to give them oral sex, but she fought back she looked at John and Mary and shouted Semper Fi and then attacked with the only weapon she had." Margie closed her eye tight for a moment then continued, "The man had a sword in his hand and beheaded her. Susan moved up behind her and put her hand on her shoulder, "He then made Janet carry it to the fire pit to be burned. After calling her John's half breed daughter!"

Janet slowly leaned forward and softly spoke, *"We will help her to forget this."*

She give her a meek grin, "I told them that if they ever get out of jail, that I pour a lot of concert and my building do not fall down very easily."

Janet looked over her shoulder at Albert and then back at Margie then at Susan as she shook her head, *"Ant hill on reservation in Arizona."*

Albert gave everyone a big smile; "I will play my bagpipes so not one can hear them scream."

Janet raised her hand to her mouth and pretended to cut off lips.

Albert let pit a loud roar, "I like that idea a lot."

Billy turned to his police cadets with a smile, "I did not hear that."

CHAPTER 36

President Betty Jones was slowly making her way to the pressroom and she was going over her notes, Senator Barbara Thomas was at her side and looked ill. "Madam, you will have my resignation on your desk by the end of tomorrow."

President Jones s looked up from her notes, "I will not except it, I need you in the senate more then ever. We will let the voters decide if you stay or leave."

One of President's aides met her just outside the door to the pressroom with a makeup case but she just held up her hand, "Not today, Lisa."

Inside of the pressroom, Carol Beckman was standing in front of members of the press. "Please be seated the President will be addressing the media at this emergency shortly and no one in the white house has slept for a couple of days."

One of the members of the press pointed toward a covered easel off to the side of the podium with a Marine standing guard, "What is under that?"

Carol looked at the easel for a moment and replied, "Hell on earth."

The President, Vice President, Senators and Marine Brigade General Artie Goodman walked into the room and headed toward the stage. The President walked up to the podium and the rest stood behind the President. She looked around the pressroom and then down at her notes, "I wish I could say good morning, but it is not. Three days ago I was informed that President Chavez of Enceladus was killed and his staff were arrested or shot. The officers that were not loyal to Chavez went to the main jailhouse and swore in Angella Romani as acting President, until they could hold a free election. Once she was swore in she was inform of a prison camp nick named Camp HELL that housed over 400 men, women and children." She took a deep breath; "Also in this camp are three Americans, one a United State Marine he was a Navy seal for close to nineteen years. After confirming his identity I ordered the U.S.S Nokomis and the hospital ship Mercy to head to Enceladus." She paused and took another deep breath. "Yesterday afternoon using classified

assets that were available to use we understood
that the prisoners were going to fight back, which
would have resulted in several lives lost, so a Navy
Seal team volunteered to parachute in and
rendezvous with the prisoners. She turned to look
at Senator Barbara Thomas who just nodded her
head as she wiped a tear from her face, one of the
other Senators put his hand on her shoulder. "With
the help of the Enceladus Military a diversion was
set up as the Navy Seal's and a female Corpsman
parachuted in and within minutes the Corpsman
was doing an emergence appendectomy on a little
girl who could not wait until rescue." She looked at
her notes and then back up with worried, "This
morning at sunrise, President Romani ordered the
guards to surrender. What she did not tell them
was that some attacking forces were close by if they
did not. They did not, and started to shoot toward
prisoners and destroying evidence! Within
seconds the attacking forces were on the ground
and in the air eliminating the threat and getting the
prisoners out as fast as they could." Again, she
looked up from her notes, "This is an ongoing
operation so I cannot give you more details now,
those that were shot, or injured are getting medical
treatment on the Mercy. Brigade General Goodman
will fill you in on what he knows I will not answers
any questions now, let' all take a moment for all the
prisoners that are now on the Mercy, and the
Marines who went in and got them." Everyone
bowed their head in silence for a minute or so and
then without another word she turned and left the

room with Vice President Cook and the members of congress.

Goodman pulled out a pointer and nodded to the Marine next to the easel who uncovered a large aerial picture of the camp. He walked up to point out key spots, "This is a picture of Camp Hell, before the raid." Then he pointed to a dilapidated structure, "This building is where the prisoners were being held and as you can see it has a large hole in the roof. This is where the Navy Seals parachuted into the complex. The buildings over here are where the guards slept and the other one is where they kelp all of the records of what happened in the camp even video's." He moved the pointer around the perimeter of the camp, "All around the camp is a mine field, that is why we needed to used helicopters and not ground forces. The only road leading into the camp had mines on both sides and is a half mine long, the two towers at the main gate have machine guns."

Goodman then walked over to the podium, "I will have a update at 5 pm today at the pentagon, and on a side note, my son is a Lance Corporal on the Nokomis, and as a parent I'm also worried about the men and women who have taken part in this operations. I will answers as many questions as I can at 5 pm." Without another word he turned and left the room.

CHAPTER 37

Doctor Sandy O'Donnell slowly make her way to post op and she couldn't believe what she was saw, over half the kids she saw had birth defects. One of the first thing she noted was that all of kids were smiling, even the ones with bad wounds and they wanted hugs and shook hands with anyone who came close. When she went to where the adults were being kelp she spotted her dad in a bed with monitors hooked up to his arms and chest, he was always strong in her eyes but now he looked frail, very pale and tired. Looking at one of the monitor she could see that he had a heart attack and she moved up next to his bed.

John slowly opened his eyes and smiled at her as he felt someone lifting his hand and he saw who it was and said in a weak voice, *"Where is Janet? I need to know if she is safe."*

Sandy patted John's arm, "I'll go and find her and bring her here so you can see her, dad." Then she saw an older man wearing a robe motioning for her to come to him she noticed he had badly bent fingers.

Doctor Mahari Guerra waited until Sandy was next to him and he then took her around the corner, "Are you Sergeant daughter, Sandy?"

Sandy could see that he was one of the freed prisoners, "Yes, he is my dad, why?"

Mahari gave her a concerned look, "This was not your dad's first heart attack I know for a fact he has not eaten or slept in over two days."

Sandy put her hand on his shoulder, "Thank, you, I need to find my sister, do you know where she is?"

Smiling at her, "She is in want the Navy calls the mess hall, we are all very hungry

"Thank you." Sandy headed toward the mess hall, but she was worried about her dad. All she can think about is how he was before, 190 pounds and always had a big smile.

It took her ten minutes to get to the mess hall because she kelp stopping to check on some of the wounded, some of the kids looked scared and she just gave them comfort. Once in the mess hall she looked around and spotted Janet sitting with two other kids who like her were slowly eating something and talking softly together, all of them were wearing oversized robes or shirts and looked unkempt. She knelt next to Janet and put her hand on her shoulder, "Janet, I'm your big sister Sandy."

Janet turned and looked at Sandy wide-eyed and put her arms around her as she started to sob, "Where is my daddy?"

Sandy just help her tight as she closed her eyes and tried not to cry, "I will take you to him he wants to make sure you are alright, but he is not feeling very good so do not be surprised when you see him."

Janet moved back a bit and pointed toward her heart, "Is it his heart that is sick again?"

All Sandy could do was nod her head and she wondered just how sick her dad ready was, took Janet by the hand, "Come on I will take you to him."

Janet reached back onto the table and picked up a small plate with a small sandwich on it, "For daddy."

Sandy just smiled as she started to lead Janet away from the table, then one of the other girls called out to Sandy, "Can we come too?" Sandy took a deep breath she gave her a smile, "Maybe later." She saw that many of the crewmembers were making sure no one over ate and that made her happy. Spotting one young boy with his head on the table looking at a plate with a sandwich and he had a large smile on his face but it looked like he might be falling asleep.

They finally reached her dad and she saw another female with a wrapped arm talking softly to him and she was extremely worried.

Diane looked up and saw Janet and a female doctor heading toward them and she smiled at them, "You must be John's daughter I have heard about?"

John smiled up at Diane and then looked at Sandy, "Yes that is my daughter, the doctor."

Janet slowly moved up to her dad's bed and handed him the small plate with the sandwich on it, "Here is something that tastes good."

John reached out and took the plate; he set it down on his lap and then took a bite of the sandwich.

Sandy tried not to look angry but saw that he had no teeth to eat with, but he still had a large smile on his face. Before she could say anything one of the nurses came up to her and grabbed her arm, "One of the female prisoners has just gone into labor and we need your help."

Diane's eyes got bigger, "That can only been Marie!"

Janet looked up at her sister with a large smile, "Can I help too?"

Sandy just grinned, "You stay with your dad and make sure he does not do anything but rest."

Diane patted John's arm, "You go and help Marie, and we will look after your dad for you."

John finished eating the sandwich and then reached out to take Janet's hand and gave it a small squeeze, "We are safe here and I want you to listen to your big sister and Diane." "Diane I want you to keep an eye on all of your students you are still their teacher until I say otherwise."

She squeezed his arm, "I know my job and you just rest and get better as fast as you can." Then she looked at Janet, "You stay with your dad I'm going to checkup on my students that are in the mess hall." She gave John's hand one last squeeze then headed out of the area and to the mess hall.

Janet looking up at all of the monitors and tube running into her father's arm worried, "Are you going to be ok?"

He looked up at the monitor and then at Janet smiled, "All of this stuff will help the doctors to make me better."

She grinned, "Then we go to America?"

John tried not to laugh as he put his hand over his heart, "As soon as the doctor let me, we will head to America." He looked up at the ceiling and then back at Janet, "When Sandy comes back I will see if I can call my wife, Margie."

Five hours later Sandy came back to her father's side and she was almost giddy with excitement, "It's a Boy, we had to put him into a Incubator as a precaution because Marie and him a good month early. But he looks good and he has a very loud voice so his lungs are good." John and Janet looked at each other and giggled.

John and Janet were sharing a cookie as John reached out and grabbed Sandy's left hand, "A Navy Seal told me that once I was safely on this ship you would be wearing his ring. Are you going to make him into a liar?"

Sandy pulled out a small box and opened it and took out the ring and put in onto her finger and held up her hand, "Is that better?"

He leaned over and gave Janet a little wink, "Yes that will do and now I need to have you call your mother so I can speak to her I need to hear her voice and tell her I love her. If you decide not to help me call her today, I just might decide to wear one of my loud Hawaiian shirts and the speedo your mother bought me as I walk you down the aisle." Janet looking at Sandy with a large smile and wide eyes, "Can I wear one of those shirt and swim suits too at your wedding?"

Trying not to laugh as she puts her hands on her hips, "Dad, you are going to wear your dress blues as it looks better on you then your Navy white and little girl, you are going to be wearing a dress!"

Janet looked at Sandy and started to giggling, "Can I wear one o those shirts and speedo's too at your wedding?"

Janet moved in front of Sandy and crossed her arms, "You had better help dad call his wife or I will not wear a dress, whatever this is?"

Sandy crossed her own arms and looked down at Janet then up at her dad, "I bet you both have been planning this, so here is the deal. I will call Mom for you, and you will wear what I tell you to wear at my wedding, deal?"

Janet slowly backed up to her dad's bed with a smirk and John just gave a little laugh, "Guilty as charged, so will you call her, please?"

Sandy moved over next to John, "Mom has never stopped loving you and she never had you declared dead."

Sandy opened her smock pulled out her cell phone and walked up to her dad. Showing her phone to her dad, "With this phone you will be able to see each other."

CHAPTER 38

Susan was standing on the front pouch watching her mother talking to the press at the end of their driveway when she heard her mother's cell phone ringing, she picked it up and saw it was her sister Sandy calling. She turned the phone on and the first thing she saw was a man face who to her surprise was her dad and she almost jumped straight up with joy, "DADDY?"

Janet had climbed onto John's bed and was looking at the phone with him, "Is that my other sister? Sandy had moved in behind them. "Yes, this is your sister."

Janet waved at Susan and smiled, "Hi, sister."

Susan rubbed her eyes trying not to cry and waved back, "Hi, sister."

John also gave a little wave, "Where is your mother?"

"She is talking to the press, do you want me to tell her that you are on her phone?"

John gave her a little smile, "Yes but I want you to do it this way."

Susan listened to John and a big smile came across her face as she step off of the porch and raised the phone over her head, "SPARKPLUG, WILDMAN ON THE PHONE!"

Margie turned away from the press when she heard Susan shouting what she and John called each other. Susan was waving her phone over her head and she started to move toward her, putting her hand over her heart, tears started to run down her face.

She grabbed the phone out of Susan's hand and looking down at it as she sat down on the porch step and saw John and Janet smiling up at her, "John its so good to see you again, I still love you my Wildman."

Fighting back his own tears, "I love you too my little sparkplug, I can't believe I am seeing and talking to you again."

Margie saw Janet next to John, "Its good to see you Janet, there are a lot of people here who want to meet you when you come home." Just then she saw Janet signing something to John.

John nodded his head at Janet and then looked back at Margie, "Janet would like to ask you some questions."

She wiped a tear from her face, "Go head and ask your questions?"

Janet moved a bit closer to the phone, "Can I have my own room and bed? Can I go to a real school too?"

Sandy reached over and put her hand on Janet's shoulder, "You can have my old room."

Margin nodded her head yes, "I'm going to get you the great bedroom set, yes you will be going to a real school as it's just out our back door."

Janet gave John a puzzled look, "Is there more to a bedroom then a bed?"

Margie tried not to cry, "Yes there is more to a bedroom then just a bed and I bet Sandy will help you pick out everything you need?"

Janet looked at her dad again and then back at Margie, "Can I call you mom?"

Margie trying not to loss it wiped another tear, "Yes you can, and can I call you my little girl?"

Janet turned and looked at her dad who just nodded his head, then back at Margie, "Yes, mom."

Margie turned and looked at her parents and John's parents trying not to cry, "Wildman, both of our parents are here and I think they would like to say HI to you as well."

John wiped his face trying to stay awake, "That would be great, but first I would like you to tell the press something for me. Tell them that I would like to thank all of the family's servicemen and women that came to our rescue. There are 384 people who will not forget them and someday I would like to personally shake their hands no matter how small or big their part was in the recue." Again he ran his fingers access his face, "Once I have talked to my parents I need to get some sleep as it has been a very long day here and I can't remember the last time I slept."

Margie stood up and walked up to Janet and Albert with a smile, "Big John wants to talk to you but he is tried and needs to rest. I need to tell the press a few things for him."

Janet slowly reached out and took the phone into her shaking hands and she saw John and Janet on the phone and she looked over her shoulder at Albert in a shaking voice, "*It's our little boy and our new granddaughter.*"

"John looked at his daughter, "That is my mother and you are named after her, and my father's Albert."

Janet gave them both a little wave, "HI grandmother, grandfather." Frank and Sue also moved behind Janet waved at them too.

Pointing at Margie's mom and dad, "That is your other grandparent's."

John smiled at them all, "Mom, Janet likes to sing maybe you can teach her some Soldier songs and dad, maybe you could teach her some Irish ballads?"

They both nodded their heads and his mother wiped away a tear and she ran her finger over the side of the phone as they all heard Sandy, "That will have to do for today, my phone needs to be charged and dad needs to rest so everyone say goodbye." Once everyone said goodbye Sandy took the phone and put it away.

John layback in the bed and with his eyes partially closed; "Please make sure everyone go to sleep in a bed and not on the floor." Within moments they can see that he has fallen asleep.

Sandy bent over and put her hand on Janet's shoulder, "Tomorrow when I'm not busy, we will start to look at bedroom sets together, but right now go back to the mess hall and I will find you a bed to sleep." Once Janet has left the area, Sandy took a picture of the ring on her finger and wrote a short message and then sent it to Anita.

Anita was watching Margie talking to the press setting with her grandfather and grandmother when her grandfather handed her his cell phone, her eyes got huge and she started jumping up and down shouting, "I'm getting a new mother!" She looked at the picture and read the message too,

"She is on the Mercy and she said yes, just before dad went on that rescue mission."

Handing the phone back to her grandfather, "I'm going to go and tell all of my friends that I'm getting a new mom."

Her grandmother tried not to laugh; "At least this will put an end to their living in sin."

Margie finished her press conference and slowly headed back to her house and looked exhausted her father put his arm around her, "When was the last time you slept?"

She smiled at him meekly, "I cannot remember, but first need to make some phone calls before I can think about sleep."

Frank shook his head no, "No, phone calls you are heading straight to bed you don't want to get sick when John is so close to coming home, so take a shower and then bed!"

Susan who had heard Frank open the door for them and said, "You heard the Captain so off to bed for the both of us."

Margie not in a mood to argue just nodded her head as she fought to keep her eyes open, "Yes, Captain." Margie couldn't even walk straight as she headed toward her bedroom. She sat down on the edge of her bed and bent over to take her shoes off which made her dizzy so she left them on and curled up and was fast asleep.

Sue took a blanket and covered her daughter up and then slowly closed her bedroom door. Once in the living room she saw Janet and Albert sitting in front of the TV watching the news about the rescue and she could tell that Janet was fighting to keep from crying, and so was Albert.

Margie went to bed and was in a deep sleep she felt like she was in a deep fog from her fatigue and in her head, hears a voice and envisions Mary all dressed in white and glowing. Mary took a step forward "I never loved your husband, I did what I had to do to keep him alive. He was the glue that held us together and we could not loss him. I was sick and could not tell your husband how sick I knew Janet would be okay, I gave Janet the gift of life and my love of music give her a hug from me and love her and help her to forget, promise me."

Margie felt the fog lifting "I promise." Just then she heard someone calling her name and felt someone shaking her.

She opened her eyes she saw her mother standing next to her bed, "It's morning and there is someone here who insists on see you. Who were you talking too?"

Trying not to laugh, "You would not believe me if I told you. Tell who ever it is to give me a few minutes to take a quick shower."

Fifteen minutes later Margie walked into the kitchen still drying her hair and the first person she saw was Chuck Brown sitting in his wheelchair and behind him was his daughter Samarth.

Chuck tried to rise a bit out of his chair as Margie entered the kitchen; "I have a business proposal for you as I don't want those bastard to get their hands on my business and use it to hire their lawyers!"

Margie got a cup of coffee and then sat down across from Chuck she saw a small stack of paper in front of him, "First I do not blame you for what your boys did, you help me a lot when I was just getting started in the construction business. Second I do not have much money left to buy your business after the one I bought in Miami last year."

Chuck just smirked and pushed the paper toward her, "Before you say No, please read my proposal, I have over 5000 employees and right now I have the FBI going over my business accounts to see if those bastard were using it to laundry their drug money."

She picked up the papers and after reading some of it, a puzzled look came over her face then looked up at Chuck, "Your company is worth over a 500 times what you are asking for it!"

He turned and looked over his shoulder at his daughter who had tears falling down her face, "I have cancer and less then a year to live at least that's what the doctors have told me. Those bastards have a 10% interest in my business and they would get it all when I die I cannot let that happen."

Samarth sat in a chair next to her dad, "They all but told me that they want me to defend them, but I said to them I can't defend drug dealers, murders and rapists."

Margie saw a pen on the table reached out and picked it up, she scratched she made a few changes to it and handed it back to Chuck, "That is what I'm willing to pay for your business and not a penny less! I also want you both to come and work for me."

Chuck looked at the papers and then showed them to Samarth with a smile, "You are so kind, I don't know what to say."

Margie stood up and held out her hand, "You are still my friend and you will be until the day you die."

Chuck pushed his wheelchair away from the table went around and shook Margie's hand, "I will get emails out to all of your new employee about you being their new boss."

Margie looked at Samarth, "My husband may need a good lawyer?"

With a broad smile, "I would love to help him any way I can."

Margie watched Chuck get into his Van and then she turned and opened the door to the garage and walked up to a large tarp. She pulled the tarp off exposing two Harley Davidson motorcycles with sidecars. She started running her hand over the handlebars of one them as she wiped a tear from her face. She pulled out her cell phone and placed a call, "Rich, my husband's bike, is just like mine, but I have only started it once a month since he has been gone and it may need some work done on it.

So could you come by and pick it up and work on it to make sure everything is running right on it."

Rich looked around his shop with a smile, "I will be there in an hour and it will be a privilege to work on your husband's bike." Setting his phone down he picked up the morning paper that has a picture of John O'Donnell on it.

CHAPTER 39

Mean while on the Mercy, Sandy was making her way through the ward checking on all of the patient some were just waking up, they the adults looked around the wad at the injured kids and you could see the comfort overwhelm them. Isabel was eating a small sandwich as she walked over and reached out to check her IV. Looking down at Isabel, "Now do not eat to fast."

Isabel put her sandwich down on her tray and crossed her arms in front of chest, "You are the forth person to tell me that!"

Sandy tried not to laugh, "We just do not want you to get sick."

She looked up at Sandy out of the corner of her eye, "Can I have another one later today and a cookie or some ice cream?"

She patted Isabel on the shoulder, "I will see what I can do." Sandy checked on a few more patients when she saw three doctors studying an X-ray and they did look happy. Nearing them she heard one of them talking, "It's her right value and I'm surprised she is doing as good as she is."

Doctor Ben Smith rubbing his chin, "If Daniela was ten pounds heavier I would say let me operate on her, but she is too weak right now, I do not think she would survive the operation."

One of the doctors also rubbed his chin "Let's see what happens over the next few days."

Smith looked at the other doctors, "President Romani will be here in a few hours and we will ask her what we should do, I do not want to make any mistakes."

Sandy put her arm on Doctor Smith's arm, "Why not ask my dad he knows her better then anyone does?" Without waiting for them to reply she turned and headed toward her dad.

John was sitting on the edge of his bed when Sandy came up to him and he could tell there was a problem. "What going on doctor?"

She tried not to look too worried, "It's a girl named Daniela, she has a bad heart and needs to have an operation, but the doctors are too scared to operate on her because she is so weak."

John saw the doctors coming up behind Sandy, he reached out and grabbed his IV pole and then looked at the doctors, "Take me to Daniela!"

Daniela was laying on her bed feeling very weak and talking softly to father Campbell who had a bandage around his head. John and Sandy walked up to her bed with Doctor Smith and doctor

Thompson in tow; John sat down on a chair next to Daniela bed. He gave Daniela a big smile, "Did you know that you are scaring some of the doctors here?"

Daniela looked at John and the doctors, "I'm sorry I did not know that but they have been running a lot of tests on me."

John held her hand, "You have a problem with one of your heart values and that is not good. If the don't fix it, you will die soon, but I told them you are stronger then they think. You have three choices, one is they will keep you comfortable until the end, two is doctor Smith here operation on you but you may die on his table and that would make him very sad. Three is he operates and you and you live for many years to come."

Daniela turned and looked at father Campbell, "Father could you do something for me?"

Father Campbell stood up and moved over to Daniela's bed, "If I can my child, I will?"

Daniela turned and looked at Doctor Smith and then back at father Campbell, "I would like you to put a bible near me and open it to the page where Jesus tells his disciples not to send the children away, while doctor Smith fixes my heart?"

Father Campbell patted her arm, "I can do that and I will be there praying for you as he operates on you."

Daniela then turned and look at Doctor Smith, "If I die on your table do not be sad I will be at the lords table, but I want to live and maybe find a new family in America."

Doctor Smith moved up to the foot of Daniela's bed, "It will take me a day or two to prepare for the operation because I need to order some special stuff for you."

Daniela just gave him a broad smile, "I'm not going any where."

Two hours later an Osprey helicopter landed on the deck of the Mercy and President Angella Romani step off. Captain Loren Ross and her mother Raeanne Romani who gave her a big hug, "It's so good to see you again and thank you for sending the Marines to save us."

Angella shook Captain Ross's hand, "Thank you for helping my people. How are they doing?"

Captain Ross giving her a large smile, "There are eight that are critical the rest of those who were injured are in fare to good condition."

Raeanne took daughter by the arm, "Before you meet Sergeant John O'Donnell or Janet we need to talk about a few thing first."

Captain Ross held out his hand, "I have a meeting room waiting for you, this way."

Once in the meeting room Captain Ross pointed at the table, "There some water and coffee, just give a shout if you need anything ease."

Both Angella and Raeanne sat down next to each other and Raeanne reached out and took her daughter's hand into hers, "First Janet is going with her father to America it was Mary's wish. Second many of the children have been asking John to help them find new families in America too."

Angella shook her head, "But she is your granddaughter and my niece? As for the children we have families who might want to adopt them?"

Raeanne looked down at Angella's hands trying to find the words her daughter would understand, "Many of children have defects that require special attention and they will need counseling for a very long time to come, and many would be scared to go back to the same country they were held prisoners in even though they are free. As for Janet she loves her dad and wants to go to America to live and go to school. Try to understand that Sergeant O'Donnell was willing to give his life for anyone and he held us together, he was always looking out for us especially the children, he make sure they ate first, and even got some education. I cannot tell you how many times he went without food so the children could eat especially the very young or the ones who were sick."

Angella smiled at her mother, "Some of the Marines asked about adopting some of the children, one even offered to give away a trust fund if I let him adopt one of the children."

Before Raeanne could respond they heard a knock on the door and a Marine Major Boyd walked in, "Madam I'm sorry for interrupting you, but I have been going over some of the records from the camp and found something that you need to know about flew in last night and have been going over some of the records from the camp and found something that you need to know about." President Romani motioned him to sit down at t he table, he had a large folder and opened it pulling out a lot of paperwork. He slid some of the papers in front of Angella, "We have discovered that President Chavez had a bank account in the Cayman Islands that has over 25 million dollars in it. His top two Lieutenants also have back accounts totaling 10 million dollars each. If you want we can start the paperwork to seize it for you, Madam?" He then puts a pen on top of the papers, "All you need to do is sign and we will get started."

Angella was in shock but slowly reach out for the pen, "I had no idea, about the money! We could sure use the money to help rebuild the country, schools, and hospitals."

Major Boyd then smiled, "We can also seize that Archaeologist bank account too if you want us too, his bank account has close to 5 million dollars in his too."

Raeanne just stared at the papers, "If I had my way that Archaeologist would be hung by his feet over a bond fire! He also indulged in some activities that on one should ever have to endure!"

Angella looked at her mother and then back at Boyd, "Seize everything he has as well, we will deal with him later and he will pay for the rest of his life!"

Raeanne addressed Angella's as she signed the papers, "I was just thinking that the kids could use some of that money for all the work they did in the fields and in the caves?"

Angella finished signing the papers and pushed them back to Major Boyd, "How long will it take the seize all of those bank accounts?"

Major Boyd picking up the papers and put them back into the folder, "Not long I have worked with the banks in the Cayman Islands before, so I have some inside contacts." He then shook both of their hands, gave Angella a salute and then left the room.

Angella turned and gave her mother a big hug, "That money sure will come in handy and I just may see what I can do for the kids too." She stood up and gave her mother another hug, "It's time I met your Sergeant O'Donnell."

They found John sitting in the mess hall having a glass of iced tea and watching some of the kids writing letter to someone, with the help of Diane.

John saw them walking toward him, he smiled as he moved his wheelchair toward them, "Madam President I'm so glad to meet you and I want to just say thank you for sending in the Marines." He turned and pointing toward the table, "Come and have a seat, let's talk."

Raeanne waited until Angella sat down, "I will go find Janet while you both talk about things."

"Madam President I do not know what to say, I still can't believe we are all free."

Angella smiled at him, "Please call me Angella, we are family after all."

John looked down at his hands, "I don't know what to say it's hard for me to talk about Mary and everything that happened."

She reached out and put her hand on top of John's, "Please do not tell my mom I told you this, but Mary was sick for a long time she needed you to stay alive."

He looked down at her hand, "That explains a lot, but it still does not make me feel good about how she died."

Raeanne entered the mess hall and lead Janet up to the table and Angella couldn't believe how much she looked like her mother did at that age. She also noted that she is wearing slippers that were tied onto her feet and was carrying some papers in her hand smiling away.

Raeanne helped Janet onto a chair and then Janet handed the papers to Angella, "Some of my friends have written some letters to you that say thank you for saving us."

Angella smiled at Janet, "I'm so glad I could help everyone and I want you to write to me once you get to America and tell me about your new home." Angella wiped a tear off her cheek and looked at John, "You make sure she does write as often as she can."

John looked at Janet and then at Angella with a smile, "You have my word she will."

Raeanne looked at Janet too, "Will you also write to me too?"

Janet reached out and hugged her, "Yes, I will grandma." She looked up at Angella, "Can my friends go to America too?"

Angella looked at Janet and then John, "That is what we were just going to talk about. Could you and grandma go and get me a nice cup of ice tea?" Once they have go, "She sure is happy today."

John leaned back a bit, "She has not stopped smiling since she talked with my wife yesterday and found out that there is more to a bedroom then just a bed. Having some good food helps too." He looked over his shoulder at the kids and then back at Angella, "Can we talk about the kids next? A lot of them would love to go to America to live but I don't even know anything about that."

Angella also looked over at the kids who were happy and full of hope. "Some of the Marines have asked about adoptions yesterday at the camp. I want to tell you that we are in the process of seizing a lot of money that President Chavez and others had in some accounts. My mom thinks the kids should get some of it for all of their work in the fields and in the caves."

John now leaned forward, "That would be a big help for all of the prisoners, as for me though I'm going to try to get my back pay so if you do get that money, I don't need it."

Angella gave him a big smile, "Seizing that money might take a while, so in the mean time we need to talk about what we should do about the kids."

He waited to see what she would want to do and didn't get his hopes up high, "Madam what I want and what you want maybe two different things, but when all is said and done it is your decision to make as to what happens to them and the money."

Just about then Janet and Raeanne come back to the table carrying a small tray with two glasses of iced tea on it and Sandy had joined them. Janet sat the tray on the table and then sat down next to her dad, "Did I miss anything?"

Angella looked at Janet with a big smile, "I was just about to tell your dad, that I'm going to call his President and see if she can help me find new parents for your friends. But you must keep this all a secret right now, we don't want your friends to get their hopes up until I find out what is going to happen, OK."

Janet nodded her head and looked at her dad, "When can I call mom again?"

Sandy moved next to her dad and put her hand on his shoulder, "Later today, but first your dad needs to have tests run and we need to start looking at some bedroom sets for your, young lady while I'm on break."

Both John and Angella pickup the glasses of ice tea and took a drink together and then John smiled, "Let me know, what you find out. And I have one more thing to tell you Daniela needs to have a heart operation tomorrow to save her life, it may not go well."

Angella set her glass down and nodded her head; "I will say a prayer for her after I call your

President today. Angella turned toward her mother, "Could you stay here until we find out what is going to happen and keep an eye on everyone for me?"

Raeanne just smiled, "I have nothing better to do at this moment."

Angella stood up and walked over to John and shook John's hand, "I will let you know what I find out as soon as I hear. But right now, I need to talk to the Captain and speak with your President."

John looked over his shoulder at Sandy, "All right doctor, let's get those test done I want to talk to my wife later about a few things I can't wait to get back home."

Sandy held back her laugher, "Okay dad, should I call the neighbors and tell them to close their windows when you start howling at the moon."

A short time later Angella was sitting in Captain Gregory Mahoney office, "Before I make my decision on the adoptions that some of the kids requested, I would like a list of them so I can check to see if they have family here first."

Gregory handed her some papers, "I have a list of all of the former prisoners right here for you."

Angella took the papers and looked them over with a smile, "Thank you, I will have my people start to check to see who can be adopted out right away."

Captain Mahoney nodded, "We are going to start giving them all eye and dental checkups later today and we have two Counselors flying in later to start evaluations. Some of them are having a hard time understanding what is going on." They both stood up, "Even after those that can be adopted are, they still will need some extra care before they head to America."

Angella reached out and shook Gregory's hand; "I cannot thank you enough for all of your help."

CHAPTER 40

Hours later Angella was standing in front of the American Embassy as a big crane put the air conditioner unit on the roof. Ambassador Flannigan was standing next to her with a grin, "You can use the other one for one for the schools we don't need two now."

Angella put her hand on his shoulder, "Thank you for that gift and if I can I would like to call your President on a secure line again and then fax her some information."

Sergeant Samarth Black came up to them and stood at attention in front of them, "Madam President could you let me know when you find out about the adoptions, I would like to adopt Abbie. I have a boy about her age and a big house; my husband is a police officer. I have already talked to him and he would love to have her come and live with us in Kentucky."

Angella walked up to Samarth and put her hand on her shoulder, "I will let you know sometime tomorrow, but you have to promise not to tell anyone about it until everything is finalized, I do not want any scams started."

She gave Angella a broad smile, "Yes Madam President, I will call my husband right way and tell him to keep quite until I tell him different." She turned and almost ran back into the Embassy as Ambassador Flannigan and President Angella head to make that call.

President Betty Jones was on the phone with Angella, "That is right we have to do this in secret until all is said and done." After she hung up, she got up from her desk it was getting late and everything was so exhausting, one good thing had happened so far, they were free now. She looked out the window thinking about how things could have turned out, how few prisoners were hurt and none were killed. She hoped it didn't take long to find the kids new homes here in America.

CHAPTER 41

Two days later John was sitting at a long table with stacks of papers and folders in front of him, some of the kids started to line up in front of him. The first kid in line was Daniela, who was in a wheelchair after her operation; doctor Ben Smith and his wife Jill were both smiling. John raised his hand and waved Daniela to come up to his table and he looked at a sheet of paper and back at her, "Your new parents live in Miami they are here today and standing behind you."

Daniela put one hand on the table as she slowly turned around and saw Ben and Jill. Daniela moved toward them and into their arms and started to cry. He held up a folder and handed it to Ben, "Here is the list of where everyone is going, do not show it to her until we are done here."

Next in line was Abbie and Sergeant Samarth Black was behind her, she started to walk toward him and he just pointed behind her, "Bring your new mom up here too." Abbie just stopped in her tracks and looked behind her and saw Samarth moving toward her.

For the next two hours John told all the kids that were being adopted where they were going and handed them the folders out with a list of where everyone was going, so they could keep in touch. Many were lining up to see their new parents on monitors all over the mess hall and some were looking at a big map of the United States with little flags on it with numbers for each child.

Little Bear walked up to John, he was getting ready to go outside for some air, "It has been a long time since I saw so many happy kids in one place."

John waved Little Bear to follow him outside and once outside they both leaned on the railing, "It's not going to be easy for a while for any of them."

Little Bear looked out toward the Nokomis, "At least they are free and have loving parents to help them get though the bad times."

John looked at Little Bear, "For the next few days I want you and the other new parents to help them all with any questions they may have and classes so they will be ready for America."

He patted John on his back, "That is one job, I'm going to love and looking forward to."

As they were talking a little girl and boy came up from behind them and pulled on Little Bears arm, "Dad, it's our turn to talk to mom."

John just watched as Little Bear was being led back inside and tries not to laugh and then he looked upward, "Sprits of my ancestors, I hope you are pleased and if you could please let me rest now and enjoy my family?"

CHAPTER 42

Days later Margie was packing for her trip to Miami. She was extremely excited to see her husband and new daughter. Stories about the kids coming to America and interview with the new parents were all over the news.

She put a sexy nightgown in her suitcase and closed it, then walked down the hall to the room that would-be Janet's; she looked at all of the new bedroom furniture. In her wheelchair next to the bed was John mother who was making sure the bed was perfect, and her mother was finishing hooking up the computer on the desk. "I have the feeling she is going to love this room, she will have everything she needs to help her with her school work."

Frank came up behind her, "I just checked and your plane is on time and I have the car all gassed up and waiting."

Susan stood behind her grandfather with her suitcase in her hands, "I'm all packed and ready to go, mom."

She turned and gave her a big smile and then looking at her dad, "Let me get my suitcase and then we will head to the airport."

Sue walked up to Margie and put her arms around her, "You give them both a big hug from us, okay."

Janet wheeled herself over and looked up at Margie, *"I can't wait to teach her many of my songs."*

From the hallway they heard Albert, "I will teach her my Irish ballads." They all giggled.

Margie then took a deep breath, "Ok dad, let's get going I don't want to miss my plane."

Later that evening Margie, Susan and Little Bears wife Cindy got out of the airport van in front of the hotel. They are met by a man in a hard hat, "Madam, I am the foreman, I wanted to tell you that we just have two more floors and then we will be done. I have everyone making sure that everything is ready for the kids when they get here. About a dozen family members already arrived and some are waiting in the lobby for you."

Margie watched as a bellhop took their luggage and wheeled it in to the hotel. She took a deep breath and headed into the hotel, she saw smiling happy soon to be parents, and many of them in tears. She Gave hugs and shook hands, "It's so good to meet you have made him and all of your kids enormously happy."

One of the men moved to the front, "Madam, my name is Jay Adam, I'm speaking for everyone here, we cannot tell you how happy your husband has make us, and you have our word they will never go hungry or sleep on the cold ground again."

She wiped a tear from her face, "My husband has told me that all of the kids are so happy that they have a hard time sleeping, they love to chatting with you all. Most are up to at least two meals a day with some snacks and they love to try new foods. With the help they will receive you will be able to buy a lot of new clothes for them. But you would have to thank President Angella Romani and all of the lawyers who have worked so hard and fast to make this happen."

As she talked more to them she found out that most were setting up trust funds for collage, they were all grateful for everything.

Margie moved around the room talking everyone and a man in a business suit shook her hand, "Madman, my name is Keith Nielsen, I'm the head of the local chapter of the rolling thunder veterans motorcycle club. We understand that you and your husband both ride bikes and we would like escort the buses."

Margie took his hand and fought back some tears; "I will let you know later today, after I have talk to my husband, but I am almost positive he will say yes."

CHAPTER 43

On the Mercy John was standing outside looking toward land, as they got closer to land. He leaned on the railing thinking about what had happened to him and he just smiled to himself. Tomorrow they will dock and then onto some buses, that will take them to the airport and then they will start their journey to America. Sandy came up next to him and leaned on the railing also, then she put her arm around him.

"Dad, I have never seen so many happy kids in one place before and Janet sure loves to sing. For a little girl she sure knows how to make up songs that everyone here wants to hear."

He shook his head a few times, "That is what Mary taught her, she would sing to cheer everyone up at night."

"I know it's hard to think about her, but she is in a better place now and I bet she is happy that her little girl is going to America."

He looked toward the sun, "I know, but it the way she died will haunt me the rest if my life, I think she would have loved to have met you and the rest of the family."

Sandy turning him around and lead him toward the doorway, "It's time for you to take your medicine and go to bed as you have a big day tomorrow."

CHAPTER 44

Margie was standing in front of a mirror checking her makeup when she heard Susan behind her, "MOTHER!" She turned and saw Susan standing with her hands on her hip. "Is there something wrong with my makeup?"

"Mother! Put on a bra! All of my friends will be watching us on TV when we meet daddy and Janet at the airport today." Susan pointed towards the bed, "Or at least put on a jacket."

Margie looked down at Susan and then stuck her tongue out at her, "Whenever your father came home from a mission I met him just like this!"

Susan stomped her foot, "But mom, there were no TV camera watching you and daddy back then!" Margie started to do as asked, "You are no fun."

Susan abruptly turned and left the bathroom and shouted, "You have one hour before we have to get on the bus."

Margie stopped short of changing and grabbed her light coat off of the bed, *"I do not care what they think or see."*

John and Janet got up from their seat on the plane after it came to a stop and John reached up to the overhead bin to grab their two backpacks. John looked toward the back of the plane at all of the kids who either had new parent or helpers getting their stuff together and he saw a lot of smiling young faces and he knew soon they would have new lives and his mission was over.

John saw Abbie with her new mother and smiled at her. Then the door to the airplane opened and a man with headphones on entered the airplane and smiled at John. He nodded his head took their bags and waved at t hem to exit the plane.

Once off the plane they see some wheelchairs heading for those that still were having trouble walking, Janet reached out and took John's hand as she looked up at him bit scared.

Janet licked her lips nervously walking down the gangway, until they round a corner and Janet saw her new mother and sister standing with their hands out to her and her daddy. She dropped her dad's hand and headed towards her new mother, Margie dropped to her knees and took Janet into her arms and closed her eyes and fight back tears "You are safe my little girl." The she opened her eyes she saw that John was also on his knees hugging Susan and Susan was also trying not to cry. She let go of Janet and stood up and moved toward John and John slowly stood up just smiled at Margie and wrapped his arms around her and held her tight giving her a very awaited and appropriate kiss, lifting her from the floor he spun her around, not caring about everyone who was watching. Susan hugged Janet and then took her hand.

Margie then whispered into his ear, "I'm so happy you are alive and back home."

John gave Margie another kiss and got onto the cart that would take them to the waiting hotel buses. He was tired and would go shopping later, and then he turned and gave all the new parents a thumb up.

Nielsen watched as the police officer pointed at him as he got into his lead car, Nielsen turned toward all the motorcycles behind him and put his fist in the air to signal startup.

He started his own bike and looked down at his daughter in his sidecar holding a Marine flag in her arms and his wife next to him on her own bike, which had a Navy flag.

As the buses pulled onto the freeway they all saw the motorcycles pull up alone side of them, all the kids waved at them and John waved had a large smile, but also was tearing up.

Janet looked at John, "Will I get to ride one of those someday?"

John just nodded his head, tried not to cry and pulled Janet closer, "It's the best way to see the country we live in."

Later after John took a shower he saw Margie standing next to the bed wearing her nightgown. He looked toward the connecting doorway to the other room that Janet and Susan were sharing for tonight, "Let's take it slow and easy babe."

Margie gave him a smile and opened the door to check on the kids and saw Janet and Susan facing each other on the two beds talking, "You two need some sleep time so lights out

After Margie has closed door, Susan and Janet started giggling, but soon they were fast asleep but first Susan looked at Janet, "Mom and daddy really love each other."

The next afternoon Paul Blue, Jimmy Johnson and Sam Miles were standing across the street in front of Paul's house lining up along with other's who severed with John. John and Margie's parents were waiting for them to come home too. The press was held off at the end of the street. The van slowly made it way to the house, Paul recognized the man in the passenger seat and he snapped to attention as he pointed to his driveway.

Paul and the others moved to the side of the van and watched as rear admiral Trent Harrison exited the van in a wheelchair followed by two young men in Navy whites wearing Navy Seal pins. An older woman and younger female wearing Navy cadet uniform followed them out of the van as well.

They all stood at attention and saluted the rear admiral as he passed then and then returned the salute; he looked over his shoulder at the younger men and back. "You remember my boys?"

Paul nodded his head and smiled at him, "YES SIR!" Paul then gave them both a smile, "Just like your old dad I see."

Rear admiral Harrison then pointed at the young girl with pride, "This is my daughter Jessica, someday she will command a Navy destroyer."

Jessica grinned, "If you say so, but I will warn you that I may just order you onto the deck and have you give me twenty on the knuckles."

Jimmy looked at the others with a wide smile, "Just like a chip off the old block"

Just then they heard Albert O'Donnell shout from the front porch, "THEY ARE TWO BLOCKS AWAY"

John was sitting in the back seat with Janet and Susan with Margie was sitting in front next to her dad who is driving, as they turned onto the street where their home was. John leaned a bit forward as he spotted a large grope of men and women all standing at attention across from his house. He put his hand on Frank's shoulder, "Stop in front of them."

Margie was fighting back some tears as she saw everyone waiting to welcome John, "Janet stay close to Susan."

Once the car has come to a stop. John opened the door and got out slowly walking toward them, then he spotted Rear Admiral Trent Harrison sitting in his wheelchair next to Paul Blue and his other two

Navy Seals buddies. Two young men were standing on each side of Harrison chair, his wife and a young female Navy cadet. John walked up to Paul and shook his hand then Jimmy and Sam, and then he approached Admiral Harrison.

Harrison looked up at his sons, "Get me out of this chair!" Both of his sons pulled him up onto his feet and John gave him a smart salute.

John saw the Navy Seal pins on each of his sons' shirt and grinned, "I see your sons are following in your footsteps Admiral."

Harrison pointed at Jessica, "Someday she will command a destroyer."

John walked over and shook his wife's hand and took Jessica's hand and turned his head kind of sideways.

Jimmy gave a little laugh, "Lookout, the spirits of his ancestors are talking to him again!"

Then he gave Jessica a hug smile and said quietly to her, "Admiral, when you are on the bridge of your aircraft carrier, try to not scare the young ensigns that bring you, your coffee."

Not sure what to say, Jessica looked at her dad and then back at John, "The Navy would never let a women command an aircraft carrier, Sir."

John started to chuckle, "The times are a changing my sprits tell me." Not waiting for Jessica to say another word John moved on to the other men and women who had lined up to welcome him home.

Jessica looked at her dad confused, not sure what to say her dad got closer, "I learned a long time ago not to question hi or the spirits of his ancestors.

What I can tell you is that if he had not listened to them many years ago when I was wounded I would not be here now or would you be, Admiral."

Jessica put her hand on her dad's shoulder and watched John handshaking hands and getting group hugs, "Let's keep this just between us, I don't want to jinx it beside I haven's t even graduated yet."

Janet held Susan's hand looked around and saw a small group of kids about her age standing next to a house next to her mom house.

Susan noticed her looking at the kids, "Those are some of the kids that live in this neighborhood, and I will introduce you to them tomorrow."

Margie was also shaking the hands she couldn't believe that so many would come to welcome him home. She saw John head toward the front porch and then led Janet and Susan toward the house.

John went to his mother and got down on his knees in front of her and took her hands into his, "Mother, I'm home for good, I'm done everything that I set out to do, the spirits have told me to stay home and raise my little girls and of course the doctors too." She snickered at him then waved Janet to come up to him, "Mother I would like to introduce you to the girl that carries your name."

Janet gave her a little smile, "Grandma you are going to teach me to sing your songs?"

She pulled Janet into her arms, *"Yes I will and your grandfather will also teach you his."* She looked at John and whispered into his ear, *"Your sprits are happy that you all are home."*

Standing behind his dad was Admiral Bender holding some papers, "Sergeant I want to tell you that your retirement has been approved you are officially inactive, and you are getting your back pay."

John put his arm around Margie, "I think I would like to invest in your company, someone told me you are having a hard time and need some new cash."

Margie responded, "We will talk about it, I have the feeling that there is a bright future ahead."

CLOSING

Later that night a guard heard another death defying scream coming from Jim Brown's cell, he walked up to his cell, "Let me guess, someone was going to scalp you or stab you or was it something different this time?"

Janet listen to her mother and smiled as she fell back to sleep as she said to herself, "Revenge is so sweet."

THE END

Other book I have written that you can find at:

<u>www.Danieldavisbooks.com</u>, all are on Amazon.com as paper back and Kindle.

Change

In the name of the king

Black Ghosts

Made in the USA
Columbia, SC
21 November 2017